Is anybody there?

Danny saw Megan inspecting the books on the Extra Reading Shelf. Biting his lip nervously, he wandered toward the back of the room.

Just then a high-pitched screech followed by the loud, forceful sound of downward-swirling water and gurgling pipes startled Danny so badly he lurched backward. If he didn't know better, he would have said it was a tidal wave coming their way!

The toilet had flushed itself!

Completely flustered, Danny spun around, looking everywhere.

Except for Megan, who was backing away from the bookcase with a scared expression frozen on her face, no one else was there.

A toilet couldn't flush itself. Could it?

And then, before Danny could answer his own question, the floor started to rumble as the superswirling, garbage-grinding, tidal-waving toilet flushed itself again.

Beware of the
Haunted Toilet

Beware of the Haunted Toilet

Elaine Moore

Troll

*To those of you who have experienced truly weird
and unexplainable whistles, gurgles,
rattles, flushes, gushes, and other
strange phenomena.*
—E.M.

Chapter 1

The hot summer sun sent beads of sweat rolling between Danny Adams's shoulder blades as he stood silently watching the huge yellow earthmovers scrape and haul the red Virginia clay in front of Crossfield School. Construction had begun the first day of vacation. Soon Crossfield would have a new wing, new classrooms, and a modern cafeteria complete with an automatic pretzel maker.

Going to school in the old building had never bothered Danny, although some parents had griped like crazy. He didn't think his parents had complained, but his dad had agreed to serve on the planning committee. Mr. Adams's involvement was cut short, however, because his job had taken him out of the country recently. Now he wasn't even around to witness the excitement.

Mr. Adams was an oil rigger—one of the best in the business, in Danny's opinion. Before leaving for Saudi Arabia he'd bought the videocamera that

Danny now held proudly in his right hand.

"I'm going to miss you," his dad had said shortly before boarding the jetliner out of Reagan International Airport. He'd tapped Danny affectionately on the chin with his knuckles. "Mom and I already set up a schedule. We'll talk on the phone every couple of weeks and write plenty of letters, but I want everything important on film where I can see it. You've got to keep me filled in, Danny. Even though I won't be here for a while, I still want to be part of your life."

Danny raised the camcorder to his face and peered through the viewfinder. He pressed the red button, and the camera hummed ever so softly. In an even voice, Danny began talking into the camera's tiny microphone.

"Okay, Dad. Here we are at Crossfield. I've got my back to Megan's house. You remember Megan. She's been in my class ever since kindergarten. She's the girl who has the same birthday as me."

Besides sharing the same birth date with her, Danny thought Megan was the most fascinating girl he had ever met. From her most unusual eyes—one blue and one green—to her cinnamon-colored freckles—she had even more than Danny—to her auburn curls that bounced playfully off her shoulders, she was amazing. No one, not even Biff, Danny's best friend, knew he felt this way. It was Danny's very own secret, and he was certain that Megan McCarthy was his first true love.

"Notice how good I'm getting at panning, Dad."

Danny slowly swung the camera from left to right. "Biff's been on vacation, so I've had a lot of extra time to practice.

"Okay, I'm going to try zooming in now." He kept his shoulder level while twisting the lens slightly with his left hand.

"Oh, wow, Dad! Look at that," Danny said excitedly. "Those guys are moving the big Civil War marker. I hope they don't break the concrete."

"Are you making a movie?" Megan's voice startled Danny.

"It's a video for my dad. He's in Saudi digging for oil." Danny kept on filming, trying hard not to let his hands shake. "And he left me in charge of capturing important events."

"Oh."

From Megan's respectful silence, Danny could tell she was impressed.

Suddenly, Megan pulled on his shirt. "Who's that kid? He's going to get hurt!"

Danny cut quickly from the first scene to focus on what Megan was talking about. "Sorry about that, Dad, but there's something else we need to see."

"Do you think the workers know he's there?" Megan asked anxiously. She started jumping up and down while waving and signaling to the workers operating the huge machines.

"I don't know," Danny mumbled. "Dad, look! There's a kid climbing around in the dirt. I don't know how he got in there because no one can get past the enclosure. That's Megan doing the screaming."

The boy looked to be about Danny and Megan's age. He had short black hair and skin the color of coffee, and he was wearing dark brown pants—not shorts, jeans, or cutoffs. Nothing as ordinary as that. These pants were held up with suspenders. But that wasn't all. The boy was wearing a cream-colored shirt with floppy sleeves—it almost looked like a girl's blouse. The oddest thing Danny noticed, however, was what the boy wasn't wearing. He wasn't wearing sneakers. He had on brown leather boots, and he carried something wooden and straight as a stick in his hip pocket. Whatever it was had a shiny silver tip that caught the sun's rays like a mirror, sending them flashing into the camera and Danny's eye.

"He must be one of the workers' kids," Danny said, thinking about the boots. He stopped talking and kept filming. "Oh, good," he said breathing a sigh of relief. "Here comes some guy. See him, Dad, in the red shirt? I guess he's the foreman."

Megan stopped screaming. "The foreman walked right past him," she said. "What's the kid doing now?"

Peering through the zoom lens, Danny could see better than Megan. "He's on his stomach, climbing up that pile of dirt."

"He's going to get hurt!" Megan cried. "Can't we do something?"

The earth had started to rumble and roar as two huge machines came barreling over the hill. Danny zoomed in closer. Off to his left he caught one of the gigantic haulers creeping across the packed lot. Even from where he stood, the earth trembled beneath

Danny's feet. Surely that boy could feel it more.

Just then, seemingly caught by surprise, the boy turned. At the same time, Danny zoomed in as close as the lens could go. The boy was staring straight at him.

Danny knew he'd never forget the look of total horror that spread across the mystery boy's face. Unable to watch, Danny pushed the camcorder away from his eye. When he blinked, the boy was gone.

"Where'd he go?" Megan asked.

Danny shook his head. He couldn't believe it.

"Vanished," he said in a hushed voice.

Chapter 2

"**B**ee-elllllllll-ch!"

Danny bit his lower lip to keep from laughing out loud. Beside him in the back seat, Biff grinned. When it came to burping and other gross noises, Biff Cunningham was a pro.

Immediately, Mrs. Cunningham eyed them in her rearview mirror. From the disgusted look she shot at them, Danny guessed Biff's mother would rather be doing anything other than driving him and Biff to school to get their classroom assignments for the coming year.

It was the last week in August. The temperature had to be at least a hundred degrees, and it wasn't even ten o'clock. Worse, they'd just started out, so the car air conditioner hadn't fully kicked in yet.

Danny could hardly blame Biff's mom for being so irritable. She was expecting a baby. Danny thought she looked huge—like she could pop at any minute. Whether she was tired from trying to squeeze behind the steering wheel or from putting up with Biff, Danny couldn't tell.

"Please, Biff! I told you before. No more belching."

"Me?" Biff feigned innocence while giving Danny the elbow. "That was Danno."

Danny's mouth dropped.

Biff slapped his knee and hooted. "Gotcha!"

Mrs. Cunningham shook her head and groaned. Sometimes Biff didn't know when to quit. It was one of the few things that bothered Danny about his best friend.

Feeling sorry for her, Danny leaned forward until his chin was behind Mrs. Cunningham's shoulder. "My mom said to be sure and thank you for letting me stay over. She would have taken us to Open House Day, but she had an early breakfast meeting with a new client."

Mrs. Cunningham brushed the damp hair off her forehead and smiled wanly. "You tell your mother that I didn't mind. I had to go up to the school anyway." She leaned her head back. "Okay, Bifford. Remember what I promised last night. You behave, and I'll take you to the mall later for that new pair of Air Jordans you want."

"I hear you," Biff said, winking at Danny.

Danny turned to look out the window. They were just passing Megan's house. Danny hoped he and Megan would be in the same room again this year. He worried about that more than anything. All last night, he'd tossed and turned. Sixth grade would be unbearable if he couldn't stare at Megan McCarthy.

"For Pete's sake! This construction was supposed to be finished!" Mrs. Cunningham exclaimed, interrupting Danny's thoughts as she slowed down in front of the school. She craned her neck to see past the car stopped in front of them at the sign. "It looks like we'll have to go around the block and park in the back."

Danny didn't hear what Mrs. Cunningham was saying. Megan McCarthy's red front door had been yanked open. His heart skipped a beat. Squinting, Danny shaded his eyes against the sun's harsh glare so he wouldn't miss anything.

At the same time, Mrs. Cunningham put her foot on the accelerator, dashing Danny's hopes of seeing Megan. Whoosh!

She was still complaining as the car rounded the corner. "They promised that the new wing and remodeling would be finished by September."

"Too soon," Biff complained. "I hope we don't have to go to school until Christmas."

"Get real," Danny said as he checked under his arm for sweat marks. If he was going to see Megan today, he wanted to be perfect. That's why last night he'd asked his mom to wash his favorite blue tennis shirt. It was the same shade as one of Megan's eyes.

A few minutes later, Mrs. Cunningham turned the engine off and tucked the keys in her purse. Together, they started along the new sidewalk leading around the new wing to the front door of the school. Mrs. Cunningham entered first, followed by Biff and then Danny.

The school lobby looked like the inside of a cave minus the screeching bats. Danny recognized the principal's voice coming from somewhere.

"Good to see you, Mrs. Cunningham. Hi, Danny, Biff."

Slowly, Danny's vision cleared as he recovered from sun-blindness. "Wow. Crossfield is a disaster."

Biff's voice echoed. "It's worse than my room."

Mr. Barrie chuckled. "I apologize for the noise and confusion. The construction crews are working around the clock to keep to our deadline." He smiled at Mrs. Cunningham. "We've invited Dr. Pumphrey, the superintendent, to our dedication ceremony in October. I hope you'll be able to come," he said, as he motioned them toward tables set against the walls of the cluttered lobby.

"I think you boys can find your way to your new classrooms using the maps our Parent Teacher Organization designed," he continued. "Sixth grade, isn't it? Biff, stay with Danny. And if you'll come to the office with me, Mrs. Cunningham, we can discuss a few things in the comfort of air conditioning. The new system isn't up and running yet, but thankfully I have a portable unit in my window."

The maps were printed on bright yellow paper. Biff snatched a couple from a PTO mom and handed one to Danny, who was busy reading the names of the sixth graders silently to himself.

"Whew! What a relief," Biff said when he saw their names. "We're in the same class. Room Fifteen. Oh, not so great. We got Horrible Hamilton! But look! Fifteen is where the multipurpose room used to be. I hope they left the basketball hoops up!"

The two boys slapped hands.

A few minutes later they were dodging sawhorses, brooms, and buckets as they twisted and turned, laughing as they hurried down the hall until Biff stopped unexpectedly outside of Room Fifteen. Danny almost collided with him.

"What is it?" Danny whispered.

"Girls."

"Where?"

"In there." Biff poked his thumb toward the classroom. "They're probably talking about me."

The serious way Biff said it almost cracked Danny up. Even so, he was careful not to laugh. Instead, he nodded and leaned closer.

Megan, Su Lin, and Sophie had their backs toward them. The girls were chatting so excitedly they didn't hear the boys come into the room. Ms. Hamilton was too busy concentrating on moving little squares of paper around on her desk to notice Biff and Danny standing behind a tower of unopened boxes. No one would know that the boys could hear everything.

"Whatever you do, Ms. Hamilton," Megan pleaded, "I absolutely beg of you, on bended knee, please don't put me near Biff Cunningham."

"Why, Megan, you're quite vehement," Ms.

Hamilton said, still moving the little white pieces of paper. "Is there a good reason for your request?"

"Definitely!" Megan waved her arms dramatically. "Biff Cunningham has gigantic legions of germs swarming all over his entire body."

Su Lin and Sophie grabbed each other. "Don't put us next to him, either. He's contagious." Then they dissolved in a fit of giggles.

Megan stomped her foot. She folded her arms across her chest. "I'm serious. Haven't you ever heard of mutant viruses? If anyone is a mutant, it's Biff."

Sophie roared. "Biff Cunningham is the King of Gross!"

Danny had to hold his sides to keep from doubling over with laughter. First of all, Biff had tormented Megan and her friends all last year, so he deserved it. Second, the girls weren't talking about Danny, so he was safe for the moment.

Danny tried unsuccessfully to stop laughing as his best friend moved away from the boxes and entered the room.

"Aw, shucks," Biff lamented. "No basketball hoops? What are desks doing in here? This looks like a real classroom!"

Danny couldn't help it. He cracked up.

Whirling, Megan extended her arm and pointed directly at Biff. "Oooooooh, there IT is, Ms. Hamilton. Mr. Utterly Cool."

"Now, Megan," the teacher corrected. "There's no need to be rude."

Clearly, Megan was insulted. Her voice trembled.

"I'm not rude, Ms. Hamilton, and I really mean it when I say I don't want to sit anywhere near him."

Biff didn't care.

"Way to go, Megan!" Biff sauntered closer to their group. "Don't you know teachers always do exactly the opposite of what you want?"

Ms. Hamilton pushed her chair back and rose slowly from her desk. "I take it you're Mr. Cunningham." Before Biff could whip off a silly retort, she turned toward Danny. "And are you also a student in my class?"

"That's Danny Adams," Megan chimed in. "He lives down the street from me. He's one of our best patrols."

Danny felt himself blush. Now that he knew Megan thought he was a good patrol, he'd try harder.

Danny expected Biff to offer some smart remark, but he didn't. Then Danny saw why. Ms. Hamilton was rearranging the little white squares of paper on her desk. The squares had names on them. It was her seating chart. Immediately, Biff picked up a pen and began clicking it nervously. He was probably hoping Ms. Hamilton wouldn't seat him in the first row.

"Ms. Hamilton," Megan continued, "you can put me anywhere except next to Biff. You can even put me in there." All eyes followed as Megan pointed to the back of the room.

Ms. Hamilton raised her eyebrows. "In the bathroom, Megan? You must be serious."

Megan put her hands on her hips and stuck her

chin in the air. "I am. I would be far happier in the bathroom than anywhere near Biff Cunningham."

Danny hadn't noticed the bathroom until Megan pointed it out. Against the back wall between the Extra Reading Shelf and Social Studies Center was an open door. Inside the tiny room and in full view was a white porcelain toilet with a wooden seat. Who would believe it? A toilet in their classroom!

Then, just as Megan was about to continue pleading her case, Biff pressed his mouth to the fleshy part of his arm right above his elbow and blew. Hard. Real hard.

"Bbbbbbbbbbb-llllsssssssbbbbbbtttttt!"

The towering force of Biff's imitation fart surprised even Danny. Only a herd of elephants with a bad case of gas might have been louder.

Rudely interrupted by what could only be the loudest, most monstrous fart in human history, Megan spun around until her eyes landed on the nearest possible suspect. Danny.

Danny cringed. Instinctively, he put his hand to his chest. In a million years he'd never do that. Fart in public? In the classroom? Around girls? No way! Especially not around Megan.

Desperately, he tried to locate Biff, but his so-called best friend was gone.

Then Danny saw him. While everyone else was recovering from the blast, Biff was twenty feet away innocently inspecting the pencil sharpener!

Meanwhile, Megan glared at Danny.

Danny's heart sank. He had some real explaining

to do if he wanted Megan to believe he wasn't the one who had rudely interrupted her with a megafart.

"Boys and girls, we have a guest." Ms. Hamilton nodded at them as she walked toward Mrs. Cunningham, who had just entered the room and was now standing beside Biff. "I expect you to busy yourselves."

Self-consciously, Danny scratched his neck and swallowed. Maybe he should leave. That's what Su Lin and Sophie had done when Biff and his mother sat down at the table with their new teacher. He could wait by the car, but glancing out the window he decided that was definitely not a good idea. He'd melt like a Popsicle out there.

Danny saw Megan inspecting the books on the Extra Reading Shelf. Biting his lip nervously, he wandered toward the back of the room.

Somehow he had to think of a casual way to mention that it wasn't his fart that had blasted out her eardrums. In fact, no one had farted when she was talking. It wasn't a real fart. It didn't even smell.

Of course, he would never mention the part about the smell. Danny wasn't exactly sure what boys talked about with girls like Megan, but he was pretty certain smelly gasses wasn't a good topic.

Just then a high-pitched screech followed by the loud, forceful sound of downward-swirling water and gurgling pipes startled Danny so badly he lurched backward and knocked a globe right off the shelf. If he didn't know better, he would have said it was a tidal wave coming their way!

Before he could stop it, the planet Earth crashed to the floor and rolled, ka-boom, ka-boom-boom, stopping only when it banged against Megan's pink sneakers.

The toilet had flushed itself!

Completely flustered, Danny spun around, looking everywhere.

Not even Biff could make a noise like that. Besides, he was thirty feet away, trapped between his mother and Ms. Hamilton.

That meant . . .

Danny's mouth turned dry at the unlikely thought.

It couldn't be.

Except for Megan, who was backing away from the bookcase with the Earth at her feet and a scared expression frozen on her face, no one else was there.

A toilet couldn't flush itself. Could it?

And then, before Danny could answer his own question, the floor started to rumble as the superswirling, garbage-grinding, tidal-waving toilet flushed itself again.

Chapter 3

"Th-th-there's no one in there." Megan's face was as pale as a ghost as she pointed to the open door.

Danny had never heard Megan stutter and stammer before. Clearly, the mysterious toilet had shaken her up, too.

"Um . . . let's hope the toilet's just broken." He tried to sound confident while secretly feeling as confused as she was. "We better tell Ms. Hamilton."

"You do it." Megan's eyes stayed glued to the toilet as she inched her way backward toward the door. "I'm getting out of here. I have to find my mother. She took my sister to kindergarten."

"Wait. I'll go with you." Danny nodded nervously toward their teacher, who was still talking to Mrs. Cunningham and Biff. "We can't interrupt them. They'll probably be talking for a while longer."

Was it Danny's imagination, or did Megan look relieved?

"Thanks. With all the changes, the halls are like a

maze. All the doors are in different places, and half the lights aren't even working."

Danny pulled the folded map out of his pocket as they started down the hall. "We can go toward the lobby, but it's shorter if we go past the library."

Stepping past ladders and whirring fans, they hurried as fast as they could without tripping on the splattered canvas tarps that seemed to be lying everywhere. Now and then they stopped to check a room number against the information on their map.

"At least it's not totally dark, or we'd really be lost," Megan whispered.

"We're not lost." Even if they were, Danny would never admit it to Megan. "The library is up there. See?"

"Well, something's wrong. We passed the third-grade pod about five minutes ago," Megan answered, unconvinced. She twirled a strand of hair nervously. "And I definitely remember seeing that lopsided orange sawhorse before, but not here by the water fountain. Someone must have moved it."

"Who?" Danny frowned. He could hear hollow footsteps and soft, whispering voices, but where were they coming from?

Megan's face paled. "You're right. I haven't seen anyone for a while."

A few minutes later they rounded a corner and bumped right into the custodian, Mr. Robotcho. Megan jumped a mile.

"Boo!" he said in a friendly way. "I didn't mean to scare you."

All three of them laughed.

"What are you kids doing in here?" Mr. Robotcho asked. "This area isn't finished yet."

Danny showed Mr. Robotcho the map. "We're trying to find the kindergarten pod. Megan's mother is there with Megan's little sister."

Mr. Robotcho frowned. "Didn't you see the signs? This entire section is off limits."

Danny looked at Megan. "What signs? We didn't see any signs."

"Not only that," Megan went on, "but we heard other people, too, and somebody tried to trick us by moving that broken sawhorse. I don't think it was very nice of whoever it was to get us lost. It's spooky in here," she added, almost as an afterthought.

Mr. Robotcho rubbed his neck. "Well, I don't know what you kids heard, but it wasn't people because there's no one here."

"Well, someone *was* here, Mr. Robotcho," Danny said, pointing to clods of dirt on the floor with his toe. "Because someone tracked in this mud."

Mr. Robotcho rubbed the side of his neck. He shook his head and sighed. "Oh, yes. I've been trying to catch that kid all day. I can mop the floor clean as a whistle, and ten minutes later, it's as mud red as the Virginia clay outside. Whoever is responsible keeps vanishing."

Wide-eyed, Megan glanced at Danny nervously. Her voice trembled slightly. "We didn't see anyone with muddy shoes, but we really did hear people. Somebody was trying to get us lost. Purposely. I'm sure of it," she insisted.

Mr. Robotcho scratched his head. "Well, they sure did a good job of it. You kids are about as far away from the kindergarten as you can possibly get. You need to go down that ramp and around the library, then take the second right. Just be careful you don't brush up against the mural. The paint isn't completely dry yet." He turned to Danny. "Where are you supposed to be, young man?"

Danny tried to sound confident, but it was hard—especially when Mr. Robotcho seemed so sure that the voices he and Megan had heard didn't exist. "I . . . I have to go back to our classroom. I can find it okay. Um . . . it's where the multipurpose room used to be. It's a cool classroom. There's even a toilet in it."

"And a ghost." Megan shuddered.

"A ghost?" The custodian laughed.

"Yes. A flushing ghost." Megan sounded very sure of herself.

Danny rolled his eyes. "I think the flusher is broken." He paused. "Maybe you could fix it."

"Good luck," Megan said sarcastically. "It flushed twice, Mr. Robotcho, and the door was wide open so we could see that nobody was in there. Flush! And FL-ush!" she added dramatically.

The custodian smiled. "Don't you kids worry. I'll get rid of your toilet ghost before school starts."

After Danny left Megan at the kindergarten pod, it didn't take him nearly as long to return to his new classroom. He expected to find Ms. Hamilton still laying down the law to Biff with his mom as a witness. Instead, the teacher was alone, rearranging files in white plastic crates on her desk.

"Oh, Danny," she said, glancing up. "I assume you're looking for Biff and his mother. They're with Mr. Barrie." She picked up a sheet of paper and waved it at him. "Your patrol coordinator, Mr. Cassidy, brought this by. It's the new patrol assignments. Would you do me a favor? Since you're going to the office, would you mind leaving it with one of the secretaries?" She squinted at Danny.

Danny had seen that quizzical look on teachers before. It meant they were checking you out.

"Yes, ma'am." He took the sheet of paper.

He considered telling her about the toilet, but the expression on her face stopped him.

Danny took the piece of paper and started to leave. Unable to resist looking, he needed only a minute to find his name. All right! Danny grinned so wide his face hurt. His patrol post was on the corner by Megan's house.

He was still scanning the list, looking for Biff's name, when he heard the same strange burps and hisses coming from the back of the room. Then a loud sp-p-p-plutter erupted from the toilet.

"Young man, would you please!"

Danny spun around, and Ms. Hamilton's eyes caught his, riveting him in place. "Mind . . . your . . . manners!"

What? Danny almost fell over.

It wasn't fair! All he was doing was reading the patrol-assignments sheet and minding his own business.

Ms. Hamilton thought he'd made that spluttering noise. She probably thought he'd made Biff's fart, too. She might even think the fart was real. And now, she thought Danny was farting again. And directly at her!

What a super way to start a new school year.

Danny glanced over his shoulder helplessly toward the now quiet toilet. What should he do?

If he worked up the courage to tell the teacher that it wasn't him who had made Biff's rude fart, and assuming he didn't laugh in the middle of his explanation, what would she think?

Danny shook his head. It was hopeless. No way would she believe it was the toilet making those powerful burps and hisses. Danny might as well face it. As of this moment, his life in sixth grade was doomed.

Chapter 4

Danny waited until he and Biff were alone on Biff's back porch before he asked, "So, did you hear it?"

Biff started laughing. "A dinosaur's blast couldn't have been louder. I thought McCarthy was going to deck you, she was so mad. If she breathed fire, I wouldn't have been surprised."

"No, not what *you* did!" Danny exclaimed. "I'm talking about the bomb that exploded inside the toilet."

"What?"

"Yeah. I'm not kidding. I can't believe you missed it. It was the craziest thing. While you were stuck with your mom and Ms. Hamilton, the toilet, all by itself, slurped up like some kind of a gigantic tornado. It was gushing and spitting. It wasn't a normal flush, and nobody was in there doing it." Danny paused. His eyes narrowed on Biff. "You sure you didn't hear it? I don't know how you could've missed it."

Biff gave him a weird look. "I didn't hear it because it never happened."

Danny stomped over to put his nose practically in Biff's face. "Did too," he snarled angrily. "If you don't believe me, you can ask Megan. She's convinced it's a ghost."

Biff doubled over. "A ghost in the toilet?" he hooted. "Give me a break. I've heard of ghouls crawling out of graves, and vampires sucking your blood, but never a haunted toilet."

"Look, Biff," Danny said, getting madder by the minute. "I'm telling you, it was worse than weird." He found himself shaking just talking about it. "I bet a gigantic monster got trapped in our school and slunk its way into our classroom. Then it flushed itself into the toilet, and now it's waiting for a victim."

Biff was practically rolling on the ground, he was laughing so hard. "You're nuts," he gasped between gales of laughter.

Danny wiped the nervous sweat off his forehead. "Well, something's in that toilet, and I'm not going in there to check it out. That would really be nuts."

By the time school started, Danny had convinced himself there was no monster in the toilet—it was simply broken. Probably the noises were caused by pipes that had been rerouted during the construction process. Or maybe something got stuck in the pipes, and the unexpected flushing was the result of some suction problem. Whatever it was, Danny was certain Mr. Robotcho had already fixed it.

Besides, for the moment, Danny had something more important to worry about.

Patrols.

Now that Megan had said he was one of Crossfield's finest patrols, Danny wouldn't be satisfied until he was captain—a definite possibility since Crossfield's patrol captain had moved out of town during the summer. Mr. Cassidy may already have had Danny in mind. After all, hadn't he been assigned the busiest intersection at Crossfield? Having been presented the most awesome responsibility of his entire life, Danny fully intended to meet the challenge.

Secretly he practiced the patrol maneuvers every chance he got—whenever he could count on his mom's not sticking her head inside his bedroom and catching him. It took a couple of tries to get the videocamera positioned so the picture didn't chop off his head or amputate one of his arms at the elbow. Balancing the camera on a stack of books set on his dresser worked best. Then all he had to do was scramble over his bed and stand on the other side of the room.

Looking both brave and serious, Danny sucked his stomach in and puffed his chest out. He kept his chin square as he stared straight ahead at the camera's tiny red sensor light while keeping his arms straight out from his sides and counting lightly to himself.

"One thousand one, one thousand two, one thousand three."

In the beginning, Danny's arms hurt so badly that he could only count to a fast one thousand fifteen before his arms flopped to his sides like wet fish. Now he could last a long one thousand thirty.

The effort was worth it. He only hoped Megan noticed.

For the first day of school, Danny's mother had bought him a new green tennis shirt, the same color as one of Megan's eyes. He'd even gotten a haircut. As he stood in front of the mirror on Tuesday morning, however, Danny wasn't pleased with what he saw. The shirt had fold lines that made him look like a walking tic-tac-toe board, and his haircut was so short it exposed the white tan line across his forehead.

"Mom, look at this," he said, picking at his chest. "And get a load of my face. Everyone's going to laugh at me."

Mrs. Adams peered into Danny's face. "I can iron your shirt, but your face looks fine to me."

Danny quickly took off the shirt and pointed to the white line across his forehead. "Oh, fine. You call this fine? On a skunk a white stripe is fine."

Danny frowned. How could he have forgotten?

Rushing into the bathroom, he opened the medicine cabinet and grabbed his father's spicy deodorant. He wasn't sure how many times to rub it up and down his armpits, but he figured ten was a nice round number.

Then he pulled the freshly ironed shirt back over his head and smoothed his hair. He placed the bright orange patrol belt carefully over his shoulder and snapped the buckle in the front. He tucked in the end and, grabbing his backpack off the dining-room table, ran out the door.

He would meet Biff later at school. Right now he had more important things to do.

Danny was at his post in front of Megan's house twenty-three minutes ahead of time. If he wanted to be the best, he'd have to go the extra mile. It was something his dad always said.

As soon as the first kids approached, Danny stuck his arms out. By now, Mrs. Weatherspoon had arrived. She had been the crossing guard on this corner ever since Danny could remember. He waited until she whistled before he lowered his arms, letting the kids cross the street. Danny heard Megan's little sister, Katie, before he saw her.

"Megan, I don't have to listen to you. You're not my boss, and I *am so* going to eat my cookie."

Immediately, he stood a little stiffer as her squeaky voice grew louder and louder, coming closer and closer. His arms popped up into position, nearly knocking Megan to the moon.

"Sorry," he said, blushing.

Danny stared straight ahead, concentrating. He hoped Megan wouldn't notice that sweat was dripping from his hairline.

Meanwhile, right in the intersection, someone's mother had stopped to ask Mrs. Weatherspoon directions. That meant Danny had to keep his arms outstretched even longer. He felt as if he were holding five megaton weights. He hoped Megan was impressed.

Suddenly, Katie stopped whining and began to sniff like a dog.

"What's that stink?" she piped up in a loud voice. "It smells like garbage."

There was a long silence as Danny's face turned beet red. He could feel Katie gazing straight up into his armpit.

Finally, thankfully, Megan said, "I think it smells nice."

"Well, I don't." Without warning, Katie pushed past Danny and stepped off the curb.

"Get back," Danny growled. "Now!"

Startled, Katie jumped back, and Danny breathed a sigh of relief.

He was still thinking how tough it was being the best patrol when Megan gave him a nudge. "The whistle blew," she reminded him sweetly.

Danny let his arms drop to his sides and stepped aside to let Megan and the others cross. Watching her, his stomach lurched. He tried to follow her with his eyes but lost sight of her in the swarm of kids racing off the buses.

"Let's go, Danno," Biff shouted. Finished at his own patrol post, he'd joined Danny on the corner. He was rolling up his patrol belt and clipping it to his belt loop.

"Just a minute." Danny kept his head down, pretending to need more time to roll up his patrol belt and pick up his backpack. If Biff noticed his red face, he might say something embarrassing.

A few minutes later the two friends crossed the street and headed toward school. Their life in sixth grade was officially beginning.

What a year it promised to be!

Besides kids and teachers, the halls of Crossfield School were filled with construction workers in splattered overalls. The high-pitched whine of electric saws joined the pounding of hammers. If the first day of school was any indication, the only time the workers were expected to stop was for the Pledge of Allegiance, the National Anthem, and Mr. Barrie's announcements. As soon as the P.A. system shut off, the noise started up again. Danny wished he had ear plugs.

Ms. Hamilton was forced to shout the roll call to be heard over the noise. Danny had to hand it to her. Even with the chaos around her she got right down to business. As the kids called out their names, she pointed to their seat assignments. Megan grinned happily when Ms. Hamilton assigned her a place clear across the room from Biff. Danny smiled, too. He was across the aisle from Megan.

When everyone was seated, Ms. Hamilton mentioned the toilet.

"As you all know, this used to be the multipurpose room. Unfortunately, we don't have the basketball hoops anymore." When some of the kids laughed, she nodded in Biff's direction, giving him credit for the joke. She even smiled when he clasped both hands and raised his arms high above his head, cheering himself.

"What we do have," the teacher went on, "is a toilet."

Everyone's mouth dropped.

"Biff, would you please open the bathroom door so the class may see inside?"

If he remembered what Danny had said about the mysterious toilet, Biff didn't act like it. He was out of his seat in a flash. He gripped the knob and with a flourish, swung the door wide open.

Sophie groaned. "Do we have to share it with the boys?"

"You'll still use the main bathrooms out in the hall," Ms. Hamilton explained. "But when we have tests, it may be more convenient for you to use this closer facility." Some of the kids snickered. Danny blushed. This was personal stuff their teacher was talking about.

"Now, we need to discuss rules for using the toilet."

When the girls giggled, Ms. Hamilton rapped her desk sharply with her ruler to get their attention. "Will someone tell me why this is so funny?" When no one replied, she continued. "Rule number one: Please close the door when you are finished—"

At that precise moment, a shrill screech filled the room, followed by the sound of swirling water, gurgling pipes, and a horrendously loud sucking noise.

Biff jumped out of his seat. He waved his hands in the air. "I—I didn't do it," he stammered. "Honest. It wasn't me."

"No way," Su Lin exclaimed. She was staring through the open door. "The toilet flushed itself."

Megan and Danny exchanged knowing glances.

"Hmm. I'll have to ask Mr. Robotcho to take a look at our toilet," Ms. Hamilton said, a puzzled expression on her face.

Megan raised her hand. "Ms. Hamilton. We—er, that is Danny and I—already did."

Ms. Hamilton smiled at Megan and Danny. "Well, I'm sure Mr. Robotcho has been busy. He's had so many things to take care of this year. I'll have to remind him."

Megan looked helplessly at Danny and shrugged. Danny sighed. Now he and Megan McCarthy had something else in common besides birthdays—a mysterious flushing toilet.

After lunch, Mr. Robotcho arrived, carrying a plunger and a wrench.

Sophie pinched her nose shut with her fingers. "Oh, gross. A plunger!"

"Sorry about the little problem this morning," the custodian told Ms. Hamilton. "I checked this commode on Friday. Other than its sweating a lot, it seemed fine. Whatever would cause an unexpected flush is a mystery to me."

Everyone listened as he lifted the tank top, jiggled the handle, and flushed.

"Everything seems normal now. The ghosts are gone for good," he said, eyeing Danny and Megan as he closed the door. Megan blushed.

"Let's hope it stays normal," Ms. Hamilton said. "We have enough distractions as it is."

Oddly enough, however, as soon as Mr. Robotcho left the classroom, the toilet flushed again. When it did, the whole class gasped. It was the strangest thing. The mysterious toilet flushed three additional times that day. All by itself. Without anyone near it.

Danny rested his elbow on his desk and his chin in his hand as he waited for the final bell to ring. He gazed across the aisle at Megan, deep in thought.

Megan turned and, seeing him, mouthed one word. "Ghosts."

Chapter 5

For two weeks, all the kids in Room Fifteen eyed each other nervously. No one wanted to be the first to use the toilet. But it was a fact, plain and simple, that sometime, someone would need to use that bathroom.

It happened on a Monday.

Danny was clearing his desk for a spelling pretest when Cassandra Derringer pushed her chair back and approached Ms. Hamilton's desk to request a bathroom pass. Cassandra was shy and a bit awkward. She was one of those kids who always had to go to the bathroom before a test. If it was a big test, she might have to go afterward, too.

A hush fell over the classroom as all eyes turned immediately to Ms. Hamilton. Everyone wondered what she would do.

Ms. Hamilton arched one eyebrow and nodded toward the back of the room.

Cassandra's mouth quivered. For a moment it

looked like she might cry. Ms. Hamilton was rifling through some papers on her desk, and she didn't seem to notice. Now everyone waited to see what Cassandra would do. Danny shifted uncomfortably in his seat. He felt sorry for Cassandra, who was frozen in fear beside Ms. Hamilton's desk. Finally, Biff raised his hand. When Ms. Hamilton didn't notice, he started making noises like gears shifting at a tractor pull. Some of the kids started to giggle.

Finally, Su Lin came to Cassandra's rescue. "Excuse me, Ms. Hamilton, but none of us wants to use that bathroom," she said.

"I beg your pardon?" Ms. Hamilton appeared genuinely surprised.

"It's haunted," Megan explained bravely.

"Really?" Ms. Hamilton arched her eyebrow again. This time she looked at everyone over her glasses, a sure sign that she was losing her patience fast. "Class, I'm sure there is a logical explanation for our overactive toilet."

"Logical, smodgical," Danny grumbled to himself.

"Ms. Hamilton's right," Ann Marie Watts concurred. "They have automatic toilets in airports."

"And in some restaurants," another girl offered.

"Except this toilet isn't like those," Sophie volunteered. "Ours doesn't wait for customers. It flushes even when the bathroom is empty."

Megan leaned back in her chair and crossed her arms. "That's because there's a ghost. That toilet is haunted."

Ms. Hamilton sighed. "Broken maybe, but no

ghosts, and it's certainly not haunted. Just to show you that you have nothing to fear, I'll prove it," she said, as she marched to the back of the room.

Then, while everyone sat helplessly, Ms. Hamilton stepped inside the tiny room and gently closed the door behind her.

Ann Marie was the first to speak. "What if it's really haunted?" she whispered.

"Yeah," Tony Ameralli murmured. "What if the haunted toilet sucks up Ms. Hamilton?"

"I wonder if anyone ever lost a teacher in the toilet," Biff said in a hushed voice.

"Ms. Hamilton's super smart," Su Lin observed, trying to sound hopeful.

"Doesn't matter," Biff answered. "If the toilet is really haunted, she'll just disappear. Sluuuuuuurp." But this time nobody laughed at Biff.

Just then the toilet flushed a strangely normal flush.

"So, who's going to go look?" someone said after the sound of swirling water had died down.

Biff bounded out of his seat. He had his hand wrapped around the doorknob when Megan threw him a warning.

"You're supposed to knock on the door before you open it."

Biff didn't have a chance. He jumped back as the door swung open on its own.

"Now are you convinced?" Ms. Hamilton asked as she reentered the classroom and closed the door behind her. "And I don't want to hear another word about ghosts or a haunted toilet," she said while drying her hands on a paper towel. She stared directly at Megan before turning to Danny.

Danny shifted uncomfortably under the teacher's gaze while Megan pursed her lips, unconvinced. Out of the corner of his eye, Danny noticed Cassandra cautiously tiptoeing toward the rear of the classroom.

Just then the room filled with a mournful wailing.

"Stop that, Biff!"

"Yes, ma'am."

Danny had never before seen Cassandra this close to tears. Trembling and with a deep breath, she walked inside the haunted bathroom and shut the door behind her.

Nobody said a word. The students only watched and stared at the door. Danny didn't care how badly he had to go, in a trillion years he knew he'd never use that bathroom. Suddenly, and all too soon, the door sprang open, then closed with a loud bang.

Cassandra walked briskly to her desk and sat down with a sigh. Danny knew that she hadn't used the bathroom for anything. He didn't blame her.

"And now, our first word," Ms. Hamilton began in a clear voice.

For the next few minutes, the kids pushed pens and pencils across paper as Ms. Hamilton called out words for the pretest. The words started out simple—*blue, gray,* and *battle.* But then they began to get tricky.

Did *potato* have an "e" on the end?

Civil. Was that with a "c" or an "s"?

Before Danny had the answer, Biff jumped out of his seat. "There she blows!" he announced.

With loud splutters and splurts, the toilet rumbled and shook. This time it all but exploded!

Ms. Hamilton slammed her spelling book down on her desk.

For a moment, they all thought Biff was in trouble. After all, they'd never had a teacher who had reason to be upset with a toilet. But then Ms. Hamilton surprised everyone. Instead of making Biff move his desk closer to hers or sending him to the principal's office, she calmly took a piece of chalk out of her desk and went to the board, where she wrote down the time.

"Since certain distracting elements make it impossible to conduct a spelling pretest, and since I find myself constantly reminiscing about my summer vacation in Yellowstone, we'll discuss that instead."

Huh? Danny's forehead wrinkled in puzzlement. What did her summer trip have to do with a toilet?

"Apparently our toilet has certain similarities to Old Faithful," she said, as she drew two overlapping circles on the board. "Can anyone tell me what our toilet has in common with Old Faithful?"

They had done Venn diagrams before but never one involving a toilet. Right away hands shot up. Even Biff, who usually didn't answer questions, wanted to participate.

As Danny stared at the Venn diagram developing

on the chalkboard, he couldn't help but smile. Ms. Hamilton was trying to make them think they had their own personal Old Faithful. But if this was her way of making their toilet seem harmless, it wasn't working. From the way his classmates kept glancing toward the back of the room, he could tell they were still spooked.

Every time the toilet flushed, gurgled, hummed, or made any noise above a whisper, Ms. Hamilton stopped the discussion just long enough to check her watch and record the exact minute on the chalkboard.

"Before lunch on Friday, we should be able to draw our own flow chart," she told them. "Possibly we'll be able to predict when the toilet will flush."

Biff leaned back in his chair. "It would be a whole lot easier if I chanted a magic spell over the bathroom," he bragged.

Danny raised his eyebrows. Biff had been doing magic forever.

"Abracadabra toilet bubble. Stop making noise and causing us trouble," Danny mumbled to himself.

"That's good," Megan said.

Danny blushed. He didn't realize he'd said the magic words out loud.

Ms. Hamilton smiled. "We have a poet in our midst. How appropriate, because we need to begin working on a writing sample for our portfolio."

Danny looked at Biff, rolled his eyes, and groaned with the rest of the class as Ms. Hamilton turned and wrote "My Summer Vacation" on the board.

"I agree. It's boring," Ms. Hamilton said, surprising everyone. "However, it's a required topic. Rather than spending an entire week on this project, let's confine it to one day. Of course, if you don't finish in class you'll have it as a homework assignment."

Biff punched the air with his fist and cheered.

"We'll begin by brainstorming out loud," she said. "But be quick. We want to get this over with."

"I threw up on the the Tower of Terror at Disney World," Biff boasted. "Does it count as a vacation story if I write about the vomit?"

"Gross, Biff. Why don't you draw a picture?" Tony asked.

"Can't," Biff hooted. "I don't have the right colors."

Danny kept his head down as he wrote some words on his paper. If only he had something good to write about. Unfortunately, nothing exciting ever happened to him, and the only place his family ever went was to his grandmother's.

"We went to Gettysburg," John offered.

"Ms. Hamilton," someone in the back of the room hollered, "the toilet's starting to make noise."

Nodding, Ms. Hamilton reached for her chalk. "As many of you already know, I have a profound interest in the Civil War. I participate in several of the reenactments in our area, but we'll discuss that later. Please go on, John."

John looked over his shoulder toward the bathroom, where the toilet was growing increasingly noisy.

John's voice faltered. "A-at Gettysburg we saw lots of g-g-graves."

"We went there once." Daryl had to shout to be heard over the toilet's roar. "It was neat. I liked the cannons."

The toilet all but exploded. *Weird,* Danny said to himself. It was almost as though the toilet thought it was a cannon. He glanced at Megan. With her hand covering her mouth, her eyes seemed wider than ever.

Ms. Hamilton recorded the time on the chart. "Do any of you feel as if you've changed as a result of your summer experience?" she continued.

Megan bit her lip and gave her shoulders a little shake as if to throw off the effects of the peculiar toilet. Then she said, "My family, my brother and little sister included, went to a Shakespeare festival. Now I feel inspired to be an actress."

Danny turned to catch Ms. Hamilton's reaction. The way she was smiling, he could tell she was impressed. He guessed their teacher had forgotten that it was Megan who said the toilet was haunted.

"Danny, what about you?"

Danny covered his paper so no one could see the notes he'd scrawled. "We didn't go anywhere different."

"But his dad did," Biff shot out. "His dad went to Saudi Arabia to ride the camels."

"He's not riding any camels," Danny said disgustedly. "He's working on oil rigs."

"And I suppose you're writing your father lots of letters," Ms. Hamilton said.

"Well, some," Danny admitted. "Mostly, I'm supposed to send him videotapes of the fun stuff my mom and I do. Even if it's not so exciting, I'm still supposed to tape it. He says he doesn't want to miss anything." Danny shrugged.

The teacher nodded and smiled. "Well, we certainly can't let all that filming experience go to waste. I'll have to remember to ask Mr. Barrie if you can film our Civil War play. Such documentation will be very—"

"Ms. Hamilton!" a girl screamed. "The toilet's doing it again!"

"—helpful to all the parents who want to know what's happening in our classroom," Ms. Hamilton continued, as she noted the time on the chart.

"Then maybe they should come see the toilet," someone grumbled.

"Enough brainstorming, class," Ms. Hamilton said, ignoring the comment about the toilet. "Start writing. I'll allow fifteen minutes for your rough drafts."

In the row next to Danny's, someone's hand went up. "Excuse me, Ms. Hamilton. How do you spell Antietam?"

"Shhhh," Megan whispered. "Forsooth. I can't think."

But if quiet was what Megan needed, she was out of luck. The toilet had started to rumble and grumble.

"A-n-t-i-e-t-a-m," Ms. Hamilton answered softly, "but spelling doesn't count in a rough draft." Again, the teacher jotted the time on the chart. "By the way, Antietam was the bloodiest battle in the entire war. The Battle of Bull Run, which was fought only a short distance from here, was the first—"

The metal handle tinkled sharply against the porcelain tank, a warning that something was about to happen. Casting a sidelong glance in Megan's direction, Danny squirmed in his seat. Megan was staring at the back of the room.

"If any of you want more information about those battles and others, see me after class," Ms. Hamilton went on.

Danny could feel the vibrations under his feet.

Suddenly the kids in the back of the room jumped out of their seats. This time the noise was more than horrendous.

Fllllusssssssshhhhhhhhhhhhhhh!

Danny took a deep breath. Frustrated, he tore his draft out of his spiral notebook and crumbled it up into a wad. He'd start over when he got home.

"I'm sorry, class," the teacher said, wiping the chalk dust from her hands before returning to her desk. "I was hoping I wouldn't have to do this, but I have no choice. It's obvious we won't be able to complete the writing project in class, so I'll have to assign it as this evening's homework."

The groan that shot through the classroom was so loud it could have woken up the dead.

"This is awful," Megan complained later in the cafeteria. "And I'm not talking about the food."

Danny picked a rubbery grilled cheese sandwich off his tray and contemplated the offensive thought of putting it in his mouth. "We don't deserve this," he said. "And I'm not talking about the food, either."

"Danny's right," Sophie said. "All we did was come to school expecting an education so we could make money and buy expensive cars. And now we're being terrorized by a stupid toilet."

"I can't even sleep at night," Cassandra complained.

"Neither can I," said Su Lin. "My parents say I'm being silly. If they heard that toilet, they'd change their minds."

"I've been in three other schools," the new girl said, "and not one of them had a toilet like this."

"Stop it, all of you!" Megan said sharply.

Everyone stopped talking and looked at her.

"We've got to fight back," Megan went on. "Nobody else at Crossfield has a haunted toilet. I checked with my little sister, and their toilet doesn't flush by itself." She paused to fold her arms across her chest for emphasis. "I say if it's not a ghost, somebody ought to find out what it is and fix that ridiculous thing. Besides, if we don't get it fixed, we'll have so much homework the rest of the year we'll never get to do anything fun."

Su Lin gasped. "That would be awful."

Megan shook her head sadly. "The absolute royal pits."

Hearing the word "pits," Danny blushed ten thousand shades of red as he drew his arms tight against his body. While Megan had been busy giving her speech, he'd already decided what he had to do.

If that toilet was out to ruin their lives, then it was up to him to save them.

Chapter 6

Danny jerked his hand back. "Yikes. That water is cold."

"Are you crazy?" Biff cautiously peered into the toilet tank. "You're not supposed to touch that water. Who knows how long it's been there. And where did it come from?"

"Calm down. I didn't mean to touch it," Danny said. "It was an accident."

"Well, stay away from me, toilet fingers."

The boys had gone straight to Danny's house after school. Now they were standing over the upstairs toilet.

"What are you boys doing up there?" Mrs. Adams shouted up the stairs.

"Flushing the toilet," Danny called down to her, like it was the most normal thing in the world for two kids to spend a Monday afternoon in the bathroom flushing the toilet over and over.

"How many times do you have to do that?"

Danny jiggled the handle and pushed down. "As many times as it takes."

"Well, if you break that thing and I have to call a plumber, you're paying for it out of your allowance. Plumbers are expensive."

"How much?" Biff shouted over the flush to Mrs. Adams. Even after nine flushes, Danny noted, the sound wasn't nearly as loud as the noise the toilet in Room Fifteen made.

"More than we can afford, so cut it out," Mrs. Adams shouted. "And water isn't cheap, either."

Biff eyeballed Danny. "That explains why Mr. Barrie doesn't call a plumber."

"He doesn't have to. He has Mr. Robotcho."

"Who didn't fix it."

They waited until the water stopped rippling in the bowl before flushing it again.

"Danny!" Mrs. Adams sounded more than a little angry.

"Okay, okay."

"I thought it would be cool to have our own haunted toilet," Biff said, as he sat down on the edge of the tub. "All those weird noises made our class fun. But if it means we have extra homework every day, I say we get that toilet fixed, and fast."

Danny nodded his head in agreement.

On Friday, instead of asking the class to open their math books, Ms. Hamilton directed everyone's attention to the Venn diagram they'd worked on all week.

"According to our data, we can expect Old Faithful to flush at precisely eleven-twenty-two."

"Cool," Biff called out.

Ms. Hamilton smiled at Biff.

Sophie raised her hand. "Do you really think it will?"

"Well, there's a percentage we can attribute to chance, but we've calculated as much as possible within our limited time frame," the teacher replied. "I think we've been accurate. We've kept the same routine each day, and I've tried to limit the outside variables, so our data should be right on target."

Megan rolled her eyes. Danny didn't understand the teacher, either.

"So, what are we going to do, Ms. Hamilton?" someone asked.

Ms. Hamilton reached for her notepad. "Su Lin, would you please take this message down to Mr. Barrie's office? It's time for him to see our toilet in action."

At exactly eleven-twenty, Mr. Barrie joined them in their classroom. The students all left their chairs and crowded around the bathroom door. Of course, Mr. Barrie was in the front. Just to be sure that no one tried to escape, Ms. Hamilton brought up the rear.

Who would want to leave now? Danny wondered.

"Don't get too close, Mr. Barrie," Megan cautioned.

He looked so puzzled, Danny hurried to explain. "Megan doesn't want you to get wet. Ms. Hamilton thinks our toilet might be like Old Faithful. We talked about it when we started our writing samples. We did a Venn diagram and a chart so we could time exactly when—"

"This toilet spouts?" Mr. Barrie interrupted, pointing incredulously.

Biff hooted. "Whoosh! Like a whale."

Ms. Hamilton clapped her hands and pointed to her watch. Everyone stopped talking and leaned forward. All eyes focused on the toilet as they waited.

And waited.

And waited.

Danny couldn't help but feel sorry for Ms. Hamilton, whose face had turned bright pink. Mr. Barrie checked his watch, while behind them the clock on the wall kept ticking. The minute hand moved forward five minutes, and still nothing happened.

"Hey, what gives?" Biff asked.

Mr. Barrie turned to Ms. Hamilton and smiled. Ms. Hamilton blushed even brighter.

"I can't understand it." She sounded thoroughly puzzled. "I'm sure we did all of our calculations correctly."

"I wouldn't worry about it," Mr. Barrie said, as he closed the bathroom door and prepared to leave. "The good news is that the toilet seems to be fine. The carpenters are finished in this area, so you can all get back to work."

Ms. Hamilton laughed nervously. "We've certainly

had our share of distractions this year." She turned to address the class. "Boys and girls, you can return to your seats now and take out your writing samples. We'll discuss them before going to lunch. John, we'll hear yours first."

Reluctantly, the kids headed back toward their desks, with Danny and Megan bringing up the rear. Danny glanced one last time over his shoulder at the strangely silent toilet.

"Too quiet," Megan whispered.

Danny nodded. They'd double-checked their calculations. They hadn't made a mistake. Something else was going on.

Still wondering what that might be, Danny slid into his chair just as John went to the front of the room to read his paper. Then, as John described his family's trekking up and down the slopes of the Gettysburg Battlefield, the water in the toilet began to swirl and gurgle. When John described the cannons, it let loose with the most ferocious flush the class had heard yet.

"It's baa-aack," they sang in unison.

"How unreliable!" Ms. Hamilton rapped her ruler on her desk just as the bell rang. "Wouldn't you just know it!" She shook her head with disgust. "Lunch, everybody. Go! Go! Go!"

🚽   🚽   🚽

"Talk about embarrassing," Megan said in the cafeteria. "You would think our toilet could have at least flushed once for Mr. Barrie."

"Yeah, it's not like we wanted it to really rip like it

did for John," Su Lin agreed. "A quiet little flush would have been okay."

"My dog acts exactly like that toilet," Sophie said. "He can do every trick a circus dog can do. Roll over, sit, speak, play dead. But the minute I or my brother try to show him off to someone, he acts like a mutt."

"Hmm," Megan said thoughtfully. "That does sound like our toilet."

"You mean it won't perform according to mathematical calculations?" Su Lin piped.

"Or on cue," Megan added.

"Or maybe . . ." Danny's voice drifted slightly.

"Maybe, what?" the others asked. They looked at Danny expectantly.

Fortunately, Danny caught himself before he blurted out something that sounded ridiculous. He didn't want to say anything out loud. Not yet, anyway. He had his suspicions, but for now, that's all they were. He wasn't going to reveal his theory until he was sure it made sense.

🍸   🍸   🍸

After another night of restless sleep, Danny weighed his options. He could confide in his mother and risk having her think he was overreacting. According to his guidance counselor at school, the worst thing he could do was keep his fears bottled up. But Danny didn't know which was worse—not telling or having his mother laugh at him.

He finally told his mom everything at breakfast. Since it was Saturday, he had all the time in the world to get it right—the flushing, the gushing, the gurgling and swirling, the rumbling and whirling—all of it, exactly right. He also told her how he couldn't sleep and that in school he had a sick, queasy feeling in his stomach. He couldn't concentrate, and it wasn't because he wasn't trying. What was happening was spooky—and it was serious, too.

Danny was surprised when his mother didn't laugh. He didn't know whether she believed him or not, but she wanted to act swiftly.

"If a toilet is upsetting you this much," she said, "let's get you into another class. Isn't there another sixth grade?"

Danny nodded. "Mr. Cassidy's."

"And they don't have a toilet?"

"We're the only ones with a toilet—besides the kindergarten."

"Why is there a toilet in your classroom anyway?"

Danny's voice rose. He tried not to lose his patience, but it was difficult. He'd told his mother why half a dozen times at least. "Because our classroom is where the old multipurpose room used to be," he repeated for what must have been the seventh time.

"And did this toilet make strange noises last year?" Mrs. Adams asked.

Danny shook his head. "That's the weird thing, Mom. None of the kids remember it being haunted." He stopped for a second. "Except for Sophie. She remembers a loud bang when the band rehearsed for the spring concert. They were doing a fife-and-trumpet piece. She was playing the trumpet, and right in the middle of the chorus to 'Maryland, My Maryland' the toilet seat fell down."

Danny shrugged. "But I don't think you should count toilet seats falling. That could happen anywhere. Besides, Sophie plays the trumpet really awful, and she was trying to hit a high note. It was just like that commercial on TV."

From her expression, Danny could tell she wasn't sure which commercial he meant. He rushed to explain. "You know, the one where the butler is carrying a bunch of glasses on a tray and then this singer hits a really high note and all the glasses shatter. Champagne all over the place. Biff says that's what happened when Sophie hit the high note. Minus the champagne, of course."

"Of course," his mother said dryly.

"Only instead of glasses breaking, the toilet seat dropped. Ka-boom! I don't know, Mom. Nobody else in the band remembers, and even if they did, I say a falling toilet seat wouldn't automatically make a toilet haunted."

"Nope." His mother grinned. "If it did, we would have been in big trouble a long time ago."

Danny smiled with relief. He sure was lucky with his mom. He wondered if the other parents believed their kids.

Neither of them said anything for a while. Finally, his mother sighed. "Danny, your father's job in Saudi is only for another eight months. He is coming back, you know."

"Yeah, in May." Danny frowned. When did they start talking about his father?

"We're not scheduled to call him until the end of the month, but I suppose we could try to reach him tomorrow," his mother offered. "This is sort of an emergency."

"Cool, Mom, but . . ." Danny paused as he made the connection. "You think I'm making this whole thing up." He was almost shouting. "Instead of calling Dad, why don't you ask Biff about the toilet when he comes over to help me clean out the garage?"

He watched as his mother folded and refolded the same dish towel in a tight little square.

"I don't like seeing you this upset, Danny." She was giving him one of those deep, searching looks. "It's not healthy. And I don't have to ask anyone. I'll write a note to Mr. Barrie. He'll probably do it right away—transfer you out of Ms. Hamilton's class and into Mr. Cassidy's. You'll like having Mr. Cassidy for your teacher. Isn't he your patrol coordinator? With your father gone most of this school year, it might be nice if you had a male teacher."

So that's what this is all about! Danny realized. He could hardly believe it. She thought he was imagining the mysterious toilet's weird antics because he missed his dad. Of all the crazy ideas! He missed his dad, all right. But that wasn't causing him to invent a haunted toilet.

"Don't you see, Mom?" he pleaded. "Mr. Barrie can't transfer one kid without transferring the whole class. The rest of the kids will call me a quitter. Or, worse, they'll say I'm chicken. Please, Mom. I want to stay with my friends. We're in this together."

Danny took a deep breath and let it out. He'd rather live in fear of a haunted toilet than be transferred out of Megan's class.

Chapter 7

Biff tied the last bundle of newspapers loosely with twine and plopped it haphazardly on the stack in Danny's garage. He turned and stared at Danny for a long moment.

"What's with you?" he demanded finally. "You've been acting funny lately—like you're sleepwalking half the time. What about the other day at hoop practice? You missed every basket—and you never miss! What gives? Don't tell me Old Faithful has you spooked."

Danny shrugged, refusing to look up. "Nothing's wrong with me. Would you hurry up? I want to finish cleaning the garage before I graduate from college."

He could feel Biff's eyes zeroing in on him like two inescapable lasers. He just hoped his friend didn't suspect how he felt about Megan.

"If I didn't know better," Biff taunted, "I'd say you've got a bad case of Megan McCarthy-itis."

Bang! The broom dropped to the floor as Danny's face burned hotter than a tea kettle. "Cut it out, Cunningham!"

Biff slapped his leg and hooted. "Gotcha! I knew it! Danno's in love with Megan!"

Danny bent down to pick up the broom and let the reality of the situation sink in. The secret was out. The way he felt whenever he was around Megan was bad enough. His ears got hot, his feet felt way too big, he couldn't keep his shirt tucked in, and his hands got sweaty for no reason. Danny knew Biff would drive him crazy if Biff thought Danny really liked Megan. He had to act fast.

"I am not in love with her," he growled under his breath.

Biff smirked. "Okay, Danno, if you say so. But I know I'm right. Look at what you did on the floor."

Danny looked down and groaned in disbelief. What a dope! He'd swept the dirt into a gigantic letter M. If he'd carved initials in a heart, it couldn't have been clearer. With one big *whack!* Danny swiped at the floor with his broom, sending dust clouds spiraling to the ceiling.

"Don't bother erasing the evidence," Biff shouted gleefully. "It's too late."

Biff swatted Danny with a rolled-up newspaper. Danny gave Biff a shove, and within seconds, they were rolling around on the cement, laughing and punching each other's arms.

They were lying flat on their backs, exhausted, when Biff said, "You know, I was only messing with you. If you like Megan, that's cool. You can count on me. I'll keep your secret."

Danny nodded. That was the best thing about a best friend. You could trust him with your secrets and everything still stayed normal.

What had happened with Biff in the garage was still on Danny's mind Monday afternoon as he marched purposefully through the school hallway. Mr. Cassidy had called a patrol meeting, and Danny thought he knew why. It was to elect their new captain.

Just thinking of the possibilities, Danny lengthened his strides. Megan would be so impressed. At that moment, he couldn't think of anything he wanted more than to see her expression when he told her he had been elected captain.

Danny rounded the corner. Except for the shiny water jug on the table, the conference room was empty. He pulled a chair out and sat down next to the chalkboard.

A few minutes later, a bunch of kids crowded into the room. Laughing loudly, they banged around, knocking into each other before taking their places around the table. Whenever anyone asked about the vacant chair next to him, Danny said he was saving it for Biff. Biff would have done the same for him.

Danny glanced at the clock. He was wondering what was taking Biff so long when his friend strutted into the room, flopped loudly into the chair, leaned back, and put his feet on the table. A couple of kids started to laugh. It was all Biff needed. Now he pretended to be smoking a cigar.

Danny gave him a stern look.

When Mr. Cassidy came in, Biff dropped his legs so fast, he almost fell over in his chair. Everyone roared. Before the teacher had a chance to correct him, Biff stood up and took a deep bow.

Danny couldn't help it. He smiled in spite of himself.

"Sorry I'm late. Did I miss anything? One of the first graders dropped all of his library books," Megan said brightly, as she set her spiral binder on the table.

Danny's head snapped. His heart skipped a beat. Megan in patrols? He glanced around the room, trying to gather his thoughts.

"Have a seat, Megan." Mr. Cassidy said while drawing a street map on the chalkboard.

Biff gazed directly at Megan. "Psssst. No sweat, M&M," he said, winking. "We wouldn't have started without you."

Danny was stunned. Who did Biff think he was, anyway? A movie star?

Megan ducked her head to hide her blush, but it was too late. Danny had seen it. By the coy way she was watching Biff out of the corner of her eye, Danny was convinced that Megan liked Biff. Danny's heart thudded to his knees. How could it be? A couple of weeks ago, Megan had practically begged Ms. Hamilton not to seat her anywhere near Biff Cunningham, the grossest piece of slime on the planet.

Despair came over him. Captain of patrols was Danny's only hope to win Megan's heart.

"We don't have much time, so let's get started," Mr. Cassidy said. "Wade Humphries, who, as you know, would have been our captain this year, moved during the summer. Do I have any nominations from the floor for a new captain?"

Biff raised his hand. Danny smiled and tried to act casual. Thank goodness his friend was focusing on the election. Danny shifted in his chair. He wanted to be sure to catch Megan's expression as Biff nominated him for the most important job in the school.

"Biff." Mr. Cassidy pointed with his chalk.

"Biff Cunningham." Biff announced in a loud voice.

Mr. Cassidy scratched his head. A tiny hint of a smile crossed his face. "Yes, we all know who you are. Who would you like to nominate?"

"I told you," Biff replied stiffly. "Biff Cunningham. I nominate myself."

Mr. Cassidy cleared his throat. "Well, this certainly is unusual."

"I second!" another student shouted. A titter went around the table.

"I guess that makes it legal," Mr. Cassidy said doubtfully, as he wrote Biff's name at the top of the board.

Frantic, Danny glanced at his fellow patrols. If no one nominated him, should he nominate himself? No, he decided. Just because Biff had done it didn't mean he should do the same.

"Are there any other nominations for captain?" the teacher asked. Within minutes, Sally McDonough and Vernon Washington's names appeared under Biff's.

Finally, Megan raised her hand. When Mr. Cassidy nodded, she stood up straight as a rod with both hands flat on the table. Her voice rang out clear as a bell. "I nominate Danny Adams."

Gulp. In a heartbeat he'd forgotten the pain of a few minutes ago. He must have been mistaken— Megan didn't like Biff. Maybe she liked him!

Biff's voice brought him back. "What the heck, M&M. I'll second."

That was twice in ten minutes that Megan's face had turned fiery red. Danny groaned inwardly. It certainly looked as if Megan liked Biff's paying attention to her.

Mr. Cassidy gave each patrol a strip of paper. Using their hands to cover their ballots, they all bent over the table.

Should I vote for myself? Danny wondered. He knew the girls would vote for Sally. Girls always voted for girls. That meant eight votes for Sally and the rest of the votes would be divided between him, Vernon, and Biff.

If the boys had been smart, they would have thrown in another girl's name, just to divide the votes. Danny scowled. Did Megan nominate him to split the boys' vote? What a depressing thought.

Maybe she didn't really want him to be captain of patrols. Maybe she'd vote for Sally and not for him.

If he ended up with only one vote beside his name and Sally had eight, everyone would know he'd voted for himself. How embarrassing.

"Is everyone finished?" Mr. Cassidy asked.

They put their pencils down and began folding their ballots in half before passing them to Mr. Cassidy—except for Biff, who folded his ballot in the shape of a football. One by one, Mr. Cassidy unfolded the strips of paper and read out the names. When it was all over, Biff had won by two votes.

Danny stared at the final tally in disbelief. Sally only got one vote. Except for Sally and Megan, all the girls had voted for Biff. Judging by Biff's cocky expression, he knew it, too. Danny turned to Biff and smiled. Okay, so it was an uncomfortable smile but it was still a smile.

"If it couldn't be me, I'm happy my best friend won," Danny said gamely while shaking Biff's hand.

"Now that that's done," Mr. Cassidy continued, "I've changed a few of your patrol assignments."

Everyone leaned closer.

"Myron, I'm moving you to the corner of Davis Circle and White Horse Lane. And Megan . . ."

"Yes, Mr. Cassidy?"

"I'm assigning you to Myron's old post. The corner of Wilderness and—"

Danny was too stunned to hear the rest of it. Megan would patrol the corner across the street from Biff.

Danny held his head in his hands and groaned

silently to himself as his heart sank to an all-time low. Now every morning and every afternoon Captain Biff and M&M Megan would smile at each other across the street. Worse, every morning and every afternoon, they would pass his corner. He'd see them together walking, talking, smiling, laughing. M&M and the captain. The captain and M&M.

It was enough to make Danny puke. What had he ever done to deserve this?

Completely depressed, Danny trudged back to Room Fifteen. He shuffled over to the Extra Reading Shelf in the back of the room. The rest of the kids were in the middle of their free-reading period. Usually he looked forward to this time of the day to read a chapter or two in one of his favorite books. Not now. Danny stared at the books. He didn't feel like doing anything, not even reading. He just wanted to be left alone.

Finally, and only because Danny knew he was expected to do so, he picked up a book with a blue-and-gray cover with faded red stars. At the same time, he heard a familiar silly gurgle. The last thing in the world he needed was a haunted toilet laughing at him.

"Quit it," he growled at the toilet. He didn't bother to turn around. He didn't even bother to look up. "It's not funny."

"Gotcha!" Biff crowed, coming up behind Danny. "Caught you talking to the toilet!" And just in case that wasn't funny enough, Biff did a fast spluttery toilet imitation. Standing beside Biff, Megan covered her mouth to keep from giggling.

Danny cringed. How embarrassing. He had to get this toilet figured out. And fast.

Chapter 8

Sunday morning, Danny and his mom waited in the kitchen and tried hard not to stare at the phone or the clock. Finally, at precisely ten minutes after eleven, the phone rang. Five minutes after the overseas operator's call, the phone rang again. This time it was Danny's dad. After his mother talked quietly for a few minutes, she handed Danny the phone with a smile and left the room.

"It's making me crazy, Dad," Danny told his father. "No, not the toilet. That's something else. It's girls this time. I don't know how you're supposed to deal with girls." He knew his dad would understand because he was a guy.

His dad chuckled softly. "I'll let you in on a little secret, Danny. None of us do. Ever."

"Gee, thanks, Dad." Danny supposed it should make him feel better knowing that he and his father shared this problem, but it didn't.

"And what about that strange toilet?" his father

asked again. "Your mother's very concerned. Are you still afraid?"

Afraid?

"Heck no! You know Mom. She's overreacting. Geez."

Despite what he'd said, just thinking about the mysterious toilet made the tiny hairs on the back of Danny's neck stand up. Still, no way would he give his parents an excuse to have him switched out of Ms. Hamilton's class. Watching Megan eyeball Biff might be the pits, but not seeing her at all would be the end of the world.

"Hey, Dad?" Danny said finally. "This phone call is costing a lot, coming all the way from Saudi Arabia. I don't exactly think you and Mom want to spend your money talking about a toilet."

"If it's bothering you, talk away," his father said.

Compared to Megan and Biff, it wasn't. "It's not a big deal anymore," Danny said. "Ms. Hamilton tried to find us another classroom, but there's no place to put us except Room Fifteen. Then Mr. Robotcho came back and disconnected the toilet, only it clanged and spluttered worse than ever! Most of the kids think it's just some fluke in the flusher. No big deal. Really, Dad."

"Okay. Then put Mom back on the phone. I owe you a letter, big guy. Save the stamps!"

"I will, Dad. I'm still working on that tape."

"Please get your notebooks out," Ms. Hamilton said the next day, as she pulled down the window shades. "We're going to see a filmstrip on the growing tension between the North and the South in 1860, and I want you to take notes."

In the back of the room, Danny heard a threatening clank, clank, clank.

Apparently, Megan heard it, too, because she slipped out of her seat and shut the bathroom door, which had been left open a crack. If Ms. Hamilton noticed the clanking noise, she didn't let on. She was too busy organizing her materials near the projector. When she gave the signal, Tanya turned out the lights. At the same time, Ms. Hamilton flipped the switch on the projector.

"'A Nation in Turmoil. The Trouble Begins.'" Cassandra read the title out loud.

Even through the closed door, Danny could hear the toilet's high-pitched, lonely whine—it sounded like a scared, pathetic, wet dog locked out on a stormy night.

As the filmstrip ran on, so did the toilet.

Mysteriously, when Ms. Hamilton stopped talking, the toilet stopped whining.

Just as they were getting to the part about Fort Sumter, Mrs. Wellburn, the office secretary, cut in over the loudspeaker. "Ms. Hamilton, please come to the office to take an important phone call."

Ms. Hamilton stood up. "I'll tell Mr. Cassidy next door that you're watching a filmstrip. Please be quiet while I'm gone." She closed the classroom door softly behind her.

For a few minutes, the class continued to look at

the filmstrip. The soft humming of the projector had nearly lulled Danny to sleep when he heard Biff's voice.

"Hey," Biff said hoarsely. "Who's in the bathroom?"

Like everyone else in the room, Danny turned around. A weird, greenish-yellow light was shining through the crack under the door.

Megan quickly scanned the room. "No one's in there," she whispered back.

Before Danny or anyone else could stop her, Megan bolted from her seat. With a hard yank, she swung the bathroom door open.

In the same split second, she leaped back so fast it was almost as though she'd been picked up and thrown.

Danny's chest heaved. His knees felt like jelly. He couldn't take his eyes off the toilet. It was glowing!

Who would want to stay in a classroom like that?

No one! In a flash, all the kids ran screaming into the hallway, shrieking, shouting, and pointing. Teachers opened their classroom doors to find out what the commotion was about.

Mr. Cassidy came running out of his room and clapped his hands three times. "Enough! Quiet!" he shouted over the din. He listened as several students told him about the glowing toilet, then he charged into the room.

"Oh, no!" Su Lin wailed. "The toilet's going to slurp up Mr. Cassidy!"

"Or explode on him," Sophie moaned. She hung

on to Su Lin while Megan stood silently between Danny and Biff. She'd never admit it, but Danny could tell by the two white spots pulsating near Megan's temples that she was as scared as the rest of them.

Long, agonizing minutes later, Mr. Cassidy returned, his lips pursed together. His broad shoulders rose and fell as he took deep breaths to calm himself. He stared at Ms. Hamilton's class and frowned.

"The only thing in there is a plain old, everyday toilet," he said finally. "There is nothing flushing when it's not supposed to. Nothing is glowing." He paused to take another deep breath. "Nothing is haunted."

Then he said the one thing that bothered the class more than anything. "You're all watching entirely too much television."

"Adults always say that," Biff grumbled on their way back into the classroom.

"Yeah, what do they know?" Danny asked.

Megan pushed her hair behind her ears. She crossed her arms in a determined fashion. "When it comes to toilets, obviously not much. I think that toilet is trying to tell us something."

"Yeah," Biff said. "That it's broken."

"No. Something else," Megan said ominously. She looked at Danny. "Isn't that what you think?"

Danny gulped. Biff and the rest of the kids could laugh at him and joke all they wanted. What had just happened was serious, and at least he had Megan on his side.

"I think what you think," he said emphatically. "There's a ghost in that toilet, and it's got something to say."

Chapter 9

"Ignore the toilet!" Ms. Hamilton told the class the next morning. "I am not about to have our work disrupted by an unruly toilet and your overactive imaginations."

Megan looked at Danny and rolled her eyes.

"Now, then," the teacher continued, "back to business. The Student Council is sponsoring its first annual talent show, and I fully expect this classroom to be well represented.

"Special invitations are being sent to the local newspapers, and Dr. Pumphrey, the superintendent, will be there."

Megan raised her hand. "When is it?"

Ms. Hamilton smiled. "I'm glad you asked, Megan. Auditions will be held a week from this Thursday and Friday." She held up her hand for silence. "The actual talent show will coincide with our dedication ceremony a week later."

Biff did a drumroll on his desk. "And now for

The Great Bifferoni, the Magnificent Magician." He leaned across the aisle and pulled a quarter from Sean's ear.

"Cool," Matthew raved. "Biff's going to do his magic act."

"You bet," Biff crowed. "I'm going to win, too. What's the prize?"

"First-, second-, and third-place trophies," Ms. Hamilton answered.

By lunchtime, everyone in the school was talking about the talent show. In the cafeteria line, a kid knocked over the pretzel machine when the orange and banana he was trying to juggle landed in a bowl of chili. Sauce, beans, and pretzels flew everywhere.

"Good thing he wasn't trying to juggle chain saws," Biff snickered.

Megan cracked up.

Sitting at the end of the table, Danny overheard the conversation between Megan and her friends.

"Are you going to try out?" Sophie asked Megan.

Megan propped her elbows on the table, stared dreamily at the ceiling, and sighed. "Of course. You know how badly I want to be an actress. With reporters coming, I could be discovered and packed off to Hollywood before Christmas. Drama is my destiny." She leaned closer to Sophie. "What I have planned for the talent show is the very deepest, darkest secret."

"Then you have to tell," Sophie whispered.

Danny looked at Biff and they both shrugged. Girls!

"I do not," Megan said. "Well, maybe." Then she raised her eyebrows and smiled coyly at Danny. "I haven't exactly asked yet, but Danny is going to be my cameraman and producer."

Danny almost choked on his milk. What was Megan talking about?

"You will do it, won't you?" Megan pleaded.

He must have turned a zillion shades of red. "Do what?"

"Film me," Megan said impatiently. "Everyone knows you have a videocamera. I saw you use it when you were filming the construction of the new wing for your dad. I can't do my act without you. Say you'll do it, please."

"Um," Danny stammered. "I guess I could. Um, I mean, sure, sounds great."

It was a struggle not to jump up and shout for joy. Working with Megan on a project—at Megan's request! Suddenly, the world was beautiful again.

Not so for Biff.

"Hey, I thought you were going to be my assistant," he grumbled loudly to Megan.

"Assistant to The Great Bifferoni?" Megan pretended to gag. "That was your idea, Big Shot, not mine. I'm not anybody's assistant. I'm star quality, in case you haven't noticed. And, by the way, if you call me M&M one more time, I'll stuff your magic wand down your throat."

Megan turned to Danny, saying, "We have tons to discuss. Camera angles, locations, lighting, cues. I'll handle the script, but I'm depending on you to find the best way to showcase my many special talents."

Danny was speechless. Locations? Camera angles? Lighting? Cues? He didn't know anything about any of those things. What had he gotten himself into? Talk about pressure, he'd probably have a heart attack before the day ended.

"Are you okay?" his mom asked when Danny arrived home. She put her hand on his forehead and checked his temperature. "You're as white as a ghost."

"Forget ghosts, Mom!" Danny exclaimed. He handed his mother a flyer describing the talent show. "Megan put me in charge of showcasing her special talents, whatever that means."

"Goodness," his mother said, as she read the flyer. "That sounds like a real challenge."

"Sure is," Danny agreed. "It's all because Megan thinks I'm an expert cameraman. We'll have to compete against Biff and his magic act, and you know how good Biff is. He's been doing magic tricks for years! Last summer, he tried levitating dogs. Real dogs, Mom!" Danny paused to catch his breath.

"I saw Biff with my own two, wide-awake eyes hypnotize his grandmother's cat so she wouldn't chase birds. You know what he did, Mom? He made Fluffy afraid of birds. I couldn't believe it. This robin came hopping off his grandmother's birdbath, and Fluffy went screaming into the bushes. Biff says the only thing he hasn't mastered is cutting people in half. He's been practicing on celery."

Danny shuddered. It was a good thing Megan hadn't volunteered to be Biff's assistant. That was when he remembered.

"And now I have to call her, Mom. It's supposed to be a very private, hush-hush conversation about her secret talent. Drama is her destiny. I'm not even allowed to use the cordless phone because she's afraid of wiretapping."

His mother snapped her fingers. "Go with it, Danny," she said, pointing at him before taking the hint and leaving the room. "You'll be fine."

Danny's hand edged nervously toward the phone. When it rang, he almost flew out of his skin.

"So, did you call her yet?" Biff asked. "What did she say? Did she say anything about me?"

"No. I didn't call her yet," Danny said disgustedly. He knew what he had to do without Biff bugging him.

"Well, when you do, don't say anything dumb, stupid, or gross or she'll call you names. That's what girls always do to me."

No kidding.

When Danny hung up, he punched Megan's phone number in as fast as he could. It wasn't a pleasant thought, but he didn't trust Biff. He was liable to call Megan and make a fart noise on the phone and then call back and tell her it was Danny who had done it. And if Danny got mad afterward, Biff would only say, "What's the matter? Can't you take a joke?"

Katie answered the phone on the second ring. It barely gave Danny time to pull himself together.

"Um. This is, um, this is Danny Adams."

"So?"

Danny stared at the receiver. So? What kind of response was that? So, what was he supposed to say now? He swallowed loudly. On the other end of the phone, all he could hear was deep breathing.

"Um, is Megan there?" He hated it when his voice squeaked.

"Yes."

He waited. This was when Katie was supposed to call Megan to the phone, but she didn't. She was still breathing into the receiver.

"Um, can you get her?" he asked.

"Now?"

"Yes, now!"

Katie slammed the phone down so hard that Danny's ear began to ring.

"Me-gan!!! ME-GAN!" Katie was screaming at the top of her lungs.

"Hello," Megan said a few seconds later.

"Um." Oh, great. Now he'd forgotten what he was supposed to say.

"Oh, hi, Danny," Megan said softly.

Danny paused to clear his throat. His hands were sweating so badly it was hard holding on to the phone. "I've been thinking about the talent show."

He could almost hear Megan's smile. "I knew I could count on you. Here's what we're going to do, and promise me you won't chicken out."

"I won't."

"Promise?" Megan insisted.

"Promise," Danny said, as Megan began whispering into the phone.

Chapter 10

Danny couldn't concentrate in school the next day. Megan was going to come over to his house after school.

"I want to see the movies you made," she had said on the phone. "I need to be sure that you're as good as I think you are."

As soon as they hung up, Danny had raced upstairs and checked his bedroom for underwear. Next he'd emptied the hamper in the bathroom and dumped everything in the washing machine. He didn't expect Megan to check either place, but he didn't want to take any chances.

He'd meant to double-check the videotape, but by the time he'd taken care of the bedroom and bathroom, eaten dinner, packed the dishwasher, finished his homework, and told his mother that Megan was coming, his mom had other plans. "It's late, Danny. Up to bed—no ifs, ands, or buts!"

As promised, Danny hadn't told anyone what he

and Megan had planned for the talent show—not even Biff. The success of their performance hinged on surprise, and if the secret got out, everything would be ruined. Megan was going to recite a spooky poem. Behind her, Danny's film of the glowing toilet from Room Fifteen would fill Crossfield's huge new floor-to-ceiling movie screen—the ultimate backdrop for Megan's dramatic performance.

"Are you kidding me? I can't move that toilet all the way to the auditorium! No way!" he'd said when Megan first told him her idea.

"Let me finish," Megan countered. "You won't have to physically move the toilet. Don't you see? You can capture every ounce of its whole glowing essence on video!"

Danny fell silent as he took in what she'd said.

"I'll stand on the stage," Megan explained. "As my producer, you'll be behind the velvet curtain. On my cue, you'll bring the house lights down, then push the button that makes that huge new screen roll from the ceiling. Next, you push the Play button on the school's VCR, and voilà! The mysterious haunted toilet will glow in all its glory while I read my poem. When I finish, the toilet will make its strange, disgusting noises. And Mr. Cassidy and the rest of the grownups will never, ever be able to say again that we 'watch too much television.'"

It was a brilliant idea. And now Danny was part of it.

No doubt they'd win the talent show hands down—that is, if they lived long enough.

With Megan sitting on one of the chairs in the Adamses' living room, Danny turned on the VCR. All he'd had time to do the night before was set the tape to start where he'd filmed the construction of the new school wing.

He hadn't counted on one thing.

"I know how to work this," Megan said, and grabbed the remote. "This arrow is Reverse and this is Fast Forward."

Danny shrugged helplessly as the tape whirred.

Suddenly, Megan paused the tape. "Who is that?" she exclaimed. "Danny, it looks like your arms. But where's your head?"

Danny reached for the remote. "Give me that."

Megan started the tape again and stared at the screen. "Danny, that *is* you! That's your voice. I'd recognize it anywhere. You're reciting the patrol pledge."

Danny wanted to crawl into a hole and die. How could he ever explain to a girl that some guys need to practice patrol arm movements?

"Hmm," Megan said. "We don't need that part anyway."

"The video of the school being built would be good," Danny quickly suggested as he took the remote and pressed Speedy Rewind. It was a lucky thing he hadn't filmed himself practicing for patrols in his underwear.

"Right," Megan murmured, as she moved closer to the television. "We'll want to keep the toilet as a surprise, so we'll use the construction part for the auditions next week. The judges are sure to like it."

A few minutes later, they were quietly watching the huge earthmovers scrape dirt near the school.

"Gosh," Megan said in a hushed voice. "Now all that red clay is a parking lot."

"The trees are gone, too, and Crossfield's much bigger," Danny added.

Megan frowned as she peered more closely. "Something doesn't seem right."

"I was thinking the same thing," Danny said. "Maybe it's because the school looks so small without the new wing and the parking lot."

"No, I don't think that's it."

They watched huge haulers circle the area. In the background, a mighty bulldozer began its incline. The camera zoomed in.

"I'm zooming in now, Dad."

Danny and Megan leaned forward as Megan's voice called out urgently. "He's going to get hurt!"

But where was the kid? Danny hit Rewind and played the tape again. The kid wasn't on the tape.

"You erased him!" Megan accused.

"No, I didn't."

"Then you cut him off. Like you cut off your own head."

"No! He was there in my viewfinder."

"Well, he's not there on the tape."

Thoroughly puzzled, Danny played the tape again. "Listen," he told Megan as he increased the volume. "There I am talking to my dad. That's you shouting about how the boy might get run over. There's the bulldozer coming closer and closer.

There's the foreman. He's walking toward where the boy is digging in the dirt."

"Wrong, Danny," Megan whispered. "The boy's not there. Where is he?"

"I don't know." Danny was dumfounded.

He certainly hadn't imagined what he filmed next. He would never forget the horrified expression on the boy's face as he heard the bulldozer charging up the hill.

"Look! The picture's all blurry." Megan turned to Danny. "I don't think you were holding the camera very still. I can't see anything."

Danny stared at the television screen, completely transfixed by what he remembered. Megan was right. But she hadn't seen what he saw through the camera's zoom lens. The boy had been pulling himself up the dirt hill, dragging one leg behind him. He'd turned and paused for a split second, gazing straight into Danny's camera. Frightened by what he saw, Danny had started to shake, and so had the camera. The boy was bleeding. He was dying right in front of Danny's eyes.

How could Danny have forgotten the blood?

"Do you think there's something wrong with the camera?" he asked Megan after a few moments.

Megan shrugged. "Maybe it's the film."

"It can't be the film," Danny argued. He was thinking out loud. "Everything else on the tape came out okay." Everything behind where the boy was digging is there, he started to say. The only reason he didn't say it out loud was because it was too weird and inexplicable.

Megan sighed. "Well, at least now we know what to be on the lookout for. When it's time, you'll have to be sure to capture the whole toilet without shaking or blurring the picture. Don't worry. I'll remind you. We need the tank, bowl, lid, seat, flusher—everything! Every glowing little detail of the mysterious haunted toilet. When it starts its performance, we might not get a second chance."

The Saturday after tryouts, Biff and Danny made a pact. Biff wouldn't attempt to cut either Sophie or Su Lin in half if Danny promised not to kiss Megan during their performance. For Danny, it was an easy promise to keep. He and Megan weren't doing *Romeo and Juliet* or *Sleeping Beauty*. Danny wasn't going to kiss Megan in a bathroom, anyway.

The following Monday afternoon, Ms. Hamilton stood at the front of the room and clapped her hands. "Okay, class! You have forty-five minutes before dismissal to practice your performances. It's not enough to be well represented. We want to be well prepared."

Out of the corner of his eye, Danny caught Biff pretending to saw his desk. He turned away quickly so Biff wouldn't see him laugh.

"Have you measured the toilet yet?" Megan whispered.

"Yeah. I checked out the distance by counting footsteps. That's why I kept going to the bathroom this morning. Ms. Hamilton probably thought I was sick or something. She asked me if I needed to see the nurse." Danny flipped through his notebook. "I've got all the camera angles worked out. I know exactly where to stand to get the whole thing in."

He couldn't help flexing his finger. It itched to start filming, but he and Megan had already decided that they couldn't film during the day. First of all, Danny's mother would never let him bring the videocamera to school. Second, the toilet seemed to glow only when the room was dark. They would have to film it at night—when everyone else was home, when it was dark and he and Megan were alone in the classroom. Just them and the haunted toilet.

Danny gulped just thinking about it, and that wasn't even the bad part. The worst was having to wait until the night before the talent show to make the video. It was the only time when Megan's parents wouldn't be home, where they might see them sneak across the street and into the school. Danny would have only one chance to film the toilet, so he couldn't make any mistakes. It would have to be perfect, and perfect was hard to do.

Megan's voice brought him back. "Will you?"

"Will I what?"

"Will you listen to me recite my poem?"

"Um . . . oh, sure."

Megan grinned. "We are going to be so good."

Soon the classroom buzzed with activity. Myron had pasted black caterpillar sideburns to the sides of his face and was lip-synching some noisy rock song.

Deidra was leaping and twirling on her toes in front of the chalkboard.

Meanwhile, Biff was showing Sophie and Su Lin how to prance around and wave their arms while he put magic eggs in a bottle. Watching Biff, Danny couldn't help but frown. That wasn't Biff's best magic trick. Danny realized that Biff was probably doing the same thing he and Megan were—pretending to practice one trick but planning to do something entirely different at the talent show. Danny thought of the stalk of celery getting whacked in half and shuddered. Biff had done a lot of crazy things, but Danny had never known his friend to break a promise. He only hoped for Su Lin and Sophie's sake this wouldn't be the first time.

Danny waited as Megan closed the bathroom door behind her and stepped onto the tiny piece of masking tape he'd placed on the floor. With her poem in hand, Megan began to read. She didn't get very far. Behind her, something or someone whispered.

"Open the door! Open the door! Don't ignore me!"

White as a sheet, Megan whirled around until her nose was practically against the wooden door.

"Who is that?" she whispered back.

"Open the door! Open the door! Don't ignore me!"

Visibly shaken, Megan wobbled to the side.

Danny's trembling hand reached for the doorknob. "Should I?"

"You have to!" Megan cried.

"Open the door! Open the door!"

When Danny yanked open the door, the bathroom was empty—and silent.

The two friends stared at each other, speechless.

Chapter 11

In the distance a dog howled. A cool night breeze lifted a handful of dry leaves and sent them scurrying along the McCarthys' driveway.

Danny shuddered.

There was something spooky about his school at night. The way the big yellow harvest moon hung in the sky directly over the school building, Crossfield might as well have been a haunted house on Halloween. If they had passed a black cat or a witch on a broomstick while crossing the street, Danny wouldn't have been surprised.

"Are you sure we won't get caught?" he asked Megan for the third time.

"Positive," Megan answered patiently. "See." She pointed. "Another lady just went into the building. They use the gym every Tuesday and Thursday night to do their aerobic exercises. They'll be so busy bouncing, stepping, and clapping that they won't even notice us when we sneak past."

Danny bit his lip nervously. "We can get in an awful lot of trouble for breaking into school at night."

"We're not breaking in. The school's open. But if you're scared . . ." Megan's voice drifted off.

Danny jerked his shoulders back. "I'm not scared, okay?" he said, putting his hand on his chest, only to be amazed by how hard and fast his heart was beating. "And even if I was," he went on, "someone has to make the grown-ups realize that our toilet is haunted, so it might as well be us. I already told my mom we were rehearsing some last-minute stuff for the talent show tomorrow."

"Good. You didn't even have to lie. My parents left for the PTO meeting at my brother's high school a few minutes ago. They won't be home until at least ten o'clock. Katie and Jason are playing video games, so they won't even know I'm gone."

Megan pointed her flashlight toward her watch. "It's seven forty-five now. You know what that means? At this exact moment in time nobody knows where we are. If anything happens, no one would ever know where to find us."

Danny laughed nervously. "You mean like if we got sucked up by the toilet?"

Megan grimaced. "Could that happen?"

Danny patted his camcorder. "Nah. We're too big for the pipes. I already checked. Besides, we won't get too close. We only need to film the toilet's glow. We should be in and out in thirty minutes max."

But even as he and Megan started across the street,

he wasn't so sure. Maybe it was the long, forbidding shadows that seemed to dart in front of them as they walked. Maybe it was the warning screech of the school's front door as they opened it and the grating noise behind them as it shut—or the memory of the mysterious whispered command to "open the door" that still haunted him. Maybe it was the cool, damp air that seemed to cling to the walls or the weird aerobic music coupled with grunts and claps coming from the gymnasium.

Whatever it was that was creepy, Danny didn't like it.

Suddenly, the gym doors burst open with a loud bang! Megan grabbed Danny's jacket. "Quick, hide!" she whispered.

They ducked behind a trash barrel just in time. A white-haired lady in pink-and-purple spandex tights pranced toward the water fountain. As she bent to drink, Danny took Megan's hand. They raced down the hall and didn't stop running until they reached the sixth-grade pod.

Leaning against the wall, Danny pulled his flashlight out of his pocket and flipped it on. Megan did the same with hers. What a team!

"Let's do it!" Danny said confidently. He swept the flashlight into the room. As expected, except for the two of them, no one was there.

"Don't turn on the lights," Megan cautioned. "Remember, we have to film the toilet at its height of hauntedness. We should turn our flashlights off, too. But not yet. It's too spooky."

"Gotcha." With Megan close behind, Danny tiptoed deeper into the dark and empty classroom. He nearly knocked over the globe in the Social Studies Center before they reached the bathroom. "I don't think the toilet is glowing or we'd see a light under the door," he whispered. Even so, the thought of opening the bathroom door sent a chill up Danny's spine. He placed his hand on the doorknob, took a deep breath, and—

Whooosh!

Quickly, Danny shone his flashlight up and down the walls, probing the corners of the tiny room. Except for the toilet and the sink, the bathroom was empty. But it wasn't silent.

"Did you hear that?" Danny whispered.

"Y-y-yes," Megan whispered back. "It sounds like someone breathing."

Suddenly, the toilet handle began to jingle like a hyperactive alarm clock. At the same time, Danny and Megan realized that someone was coming their way. The person was very noisy, loudly banging metal against metal, coming closer and closer. "Mr. Robotcho!" they both whispered at once. The school's custodian was emptying the trash cans in the pod!

Rather than risk discovery, there was only one thing they could do. In two steps they jumped inside the bathroom, closing the door quietly behind them and switching off their flashlights.

In the dark, Danny struggled with the videocamera's lens cap. The bathroom was eerily cold. On top of that, his trembling fingers felt like thumbs. He only hoped he could create a film that wouldn't disappoint Megan.

"Why isn't the toilet glowing?" Megan asked impatiently.

"I don't know. It should be shining by now."

"It's not doing anything," Megan whispered. "Even the handle's quiet."

There was only the sound of Danny and Megan breathing (and Danny's heart thudding inside his chest). In that tiny, dark, tomblike space there was nothing but spooky silence.

Megan poked Danny in the side. "Maybe it's that red light on your videocamera. Turn it off," she instructed urgently. "Maybe it has to be absolutely dark for the toilet to glow."

"That's ridiculous, Megan," Danny snapped. "The red light is the camera's sensor. If I turn it off, then the camera's off. Is that what you want?"

"Yes! Then you can turn it back on when we need it."

Danny groaned as he switched off the power. Girls! To top it off, a few seconds later Megan said the silliest thing Danny had ever heard.

"Probably the toilet is camera shy," Megan rattled nervously. "It happens a lot with amateur actors. Sometimes even professionals. Do you think it knows it's supposed to be part of our talent show?"

This whole thing is stupid, Danny thought with disgust. Being in the school at night was stupid. It could get them in a lot of trouble! Being in a bathroom with a girl was stupid, too. If Biff ever found out, he'd die laughing. But the stupidest thing of all was the idea that a toilet was camera shy.

"What made it glow before?" Megan asked, as she sat down on the floor. Suddenly, her teeth began to chatter.

"Brrr. It's freezing in here. The classroom wasn't this cold."

"Do you want my jacket?" Danny asked, feeling especially gallant after the insensitive way Megan had been treating him.

"No. Then you'll be shivering. I don't want you to shake that camera when you start filming. No blurry pictures, please!" Megan giggled, but Danny still got the point.

"Um . . . maybe Ms. Hamilton has a sweater in her closet."

"Great idea." Megan opened the door slightly and peeked through the crack. "It's safe. You guard the toilet. I'll look around and see what I can find."

"Be careful," Danny cautioned.

"Don't worry. I'm taking my flashlight."

Scared, Danny sat down on the cold tile floor and pressed his back tighter against the wall. He didn't relax until Megan returned a few minutes later with a black shawl wrapped around her shoulders. "It smells a little musty, but when I layer it over my jacket it helps." She pulled the shawl tighter. "It must be really old. I think it's one of the costumes Ms. Hamilton wears when she's in those Civil War reenactments she—"

Megan didn't have a chance to finish. Just then the floor started to rumble. The toilet's handle began to clank.

Clank. Clank. Clank.

Like a warning.

Grabbing his camera, Danny struggled to his feet as a high-pitched scream filled the pipes, then stopped abruptly. Suddenly, the entire toilet filled with an incredibly brilliant light.

Thinking fast, Danny pushed Megan back into the corner. She was trembling like crazy. So was he.

"Is the camera on? Get the whole thing," Megan whispered urgently. "Here we go! This is it!"

Danny was trying to hold the camera steady while pressing the power button, but it was hard to do with Megan pounding him on the back.

As the eerie glow began to fog the lens, Danny shifted the camera down and to the right. He would have recognized the scuffed brown leather boots caked with red Virginia clay anywhere.

That was when Danny fainted.

Chapter 12

Danny woke, looking into a set of coal black eyes. His head was cradled so softly in the strange boy's arm that he could have been resting on a cloud.

The boy motioned toward the open bathroom door. "Your friend's out searching for help. She said something about some womenfolk dancing down the hall," he explained, as he tilted a canteen near Danny's mouth.

Danny tried shaking himself awake, his thoughts speeding like wildfire. *Womenfolk? Who is this kid anyway? What's he talking about? And what's the matter with this water? Oh, no!*

Danny started to choke and sat up quickly. He wiped the side of his mouth with the back of his hand. "That water isn't from the . . ."

The boy's eyes twinkled. The expression on his face had been one of seriousness and concern, but now he was clearly amused. "From your water hole?" He laughed. "Nah. This here water's from a nearby crick."

Danny frowned. Crick? "There's no creek around here."

"Not anymore," the boy said. "It's underground now."

Danny blinked. As close as they were, he should have been able to feel the boy's breath. At the very least, he should be able to see him breathe.

But he couldn't. He was scared to think what that might mean.

Slowly, Danny stretched his arm out. If his hand went through what he was seeing, then he would know for a fact. "Don't!" The boy jerked back out of reach just as Megan returned.

"Danny! Thank goodness you're alive!" Megan exclaimed when she saw him sitting up in the bathroom. "You were out cold for so long, I didn't know what to do. It's a good thing he showed up when he did." Megan nodded at the boy sitting beside Danny on the floor.

In vain, Danny tried signaling Megan with his eyes that this boy wasn't what he appeared to be. But apparently she was too relieved at finding Danny conscious to notice anything as subtle as his eye signals.

"All the aerobics ladies left," Megan continued breathlessly. "I couldn't find Mr. Robotcho, and I couldn't use the telephone in the office, either. The door was locked. I was just about to run home to call for help, but then I thought I should come back and check on you first."

Megan reached out and touched the knot

growing on Danny's forehead. "Are you okay?"

Danny winced. "I must have hit my head on the toilet, but I'm fine now." He felt around on the floor. "Hey! Where's my camera?"

"This thing here?" the boy said, handing the videocamera to Danny. "I grabbed it before you fell. Sure is something how you can peep through that little window and see things. I looked at your water hole real good. I was pressing that red button. I figured it had to be important the way you two were carrying on."

Danny understood—the boy had peered through the camcorder's viewfinder and continued filming the toilet.

Megan sighed impatiently. "I just hope that between the two of you we got the whole toilet on video. It was so cool, Danny. Too bad you missed it. Honestly, the toilet lit up brighter than a spotlight. We'd never in a million years get it to glow like that again."

It was weird. Megan didn't seem alarmed at all by the boy's unexpected appearance.

Danny peered curiously at the boy. "I guess I should thank you," he said haltingly.

The boy shrugged. "No need."

Megan cocked her head. "You look familiar. Do we know you?"

"He's the same kid we saw on the construction site the day I was making the movie for my dad," Danny interrupted. He cleared his throat loudly, hoping Megan would take the hint. "Uh, you know.

The one who disappeared into thin air."

"Right." Megan blinked at Danny. "He's the kid you forgot to video." She turned back to the boy. "Hi. I'm Megan. You must be new this year."

The boy chuckled. He glanced down at himself, then back up at Megan. "Nah." He shook his head. "I'm hardly new."

Danny raised his eyes toward the ceiling, completely frustrated. He couldn't understand it. Didn't Megan notice the way the boy was dressed? The last time he'd seen clothes like that was in the filmstrip Ms. Hamilton showed them on the Civil War.

Good grief! Danny caught himself, startled by his own sudden revelation. Was it possible? Was this kid a Civil War ghost?

Megan rattled on, oblivious to everything. "You must be rehearsing. Am I right?"

Now Danny realized that Megan thought the boy was in the talent show and that his clothes were part of his costume.

The boy grinned at Danny, noticing his discomfort. "Got no need to rehearse."

"No?" Megan stepped back. She stared hard at the boy. "Hey, whose class are you in?" For the first time, she sounded suspicious as she eyed the brown pants and suspenders, the loose cotton shirt, the muddy work boots. Her mouth started slowly to drop.

The boy's fists clenched. "This class here is my class," he stated emphatically.

"Ohmygosh!" Megan gasped and stepped back farther. She looked at Danny and pointed. "He . . . he . . . he's the ghost!"

For a long minute, neither Danny nor Megan said anything. What do you say to a ghost? Talking about ghosts was completely different from coming face to face with the real thing.

Megan couldn't help herself. She stretched her hand out, needing to touch. Quickly, the boy moved to the side, out of reach.

"Megan!" Danny threw her a warning glance and struggled to stand up. He was now vaguely aware that ghosts might have their own set of manners, much as people do.

"We're sorry for trying to touch you," he told the ghost.

"That's all right. I figured you didn't know."

"Yeah," Danny said. "We never met a ghost before."

Recovering quickly, Megan put her hand on her hip and squinted at the ghost. "I'll bet you moved the paint cans and ladders and spackle stuff on Open House Day so Danny and I got lost," she stated. "Who are you, anyway?"

"My name is Joshua," the ghost answered calmly. "I'm sorry you got lost that day, but my spirit friends planned to ruin your school. I had to get you on safer ground."

"Why would they want to trash our school?" Danny asked.

Joshua's ebony eyes filled with sadness. "It's

because of what used to be here," he said softly.

"Huh?"

Joshua blinked. "There's no way you'd have of knowing." His voice drifted off for a moment before growing loud again. "There used to be a white house with green shutters and a broad gray porch with a swing standing where the new part of your school is now. The house was across the field from where the Union Army met Johnny Reb the third summer of the war. After the skirmish, some of the wounded soldiers got tended to on the porch. Some of the boys who were badly hurt got carried inside on stretchers on account of the flies and heat. It wasn't a hospital, but that day it was all to be had."

"I'm sorry," Megan said quietly. "You're right. We didn't know."

"But that was a long time ago," Danny interrupted. "What does all that have to do with our school or your friends?"

"A lot of my friends died that miserable day." Joshua's voice trembled as he talked. "Their spirits claimed that spot as their special place. Even when the house came to ruin, those poor lost spirits stayed on. They were peaceful and quiet over toward the gully until your big, loud, belching machines came along, pulling up dirt and shuffling everything around to put up your new building. The machines uprooted our special place. My friends were angry. You never heard such wailing as they planned their revenge. I kept you safe by making you walk in circles until they came to their senses."

"Thank you. That was very kind of you," Megan said. "Did your spirit friends find another special place nearby?" she asked softly.

Joshua sighed. "Mostly they're making do."

"But you're still here." Megan giggled. "And causing quite a fuss, if I may say so. Not that it hasn't been fun," she added as she poked Danny in the side with her elbow.

"Wait a second, Joshua," Danny said, blocking Megan's elbow with his arm. "Can anybody else see you besides me and Megan?"

Joshua shook his head. "No. We ghosts have to be careful. We only show ourselves to those flesh-and-bloods we trust."

Flesh-and-bloods must be people, alive people, Danny mused. "And of all the people you could have shown yourself to, why did you trust us?"

"'Cause I was born on November tenth," Joshua answered quickly.

Megan and Danny looked at each other. "That's our birthday," they said at the same time.

Joshua thumped his chest. "Same as me."

There had to be more. Danny knew from movies and books that ghosts usually have a good reason for showing themselves to people—er, flesh-and-bloods. It had to be more than a shared birthday that kept him and Megan safe from a ghost attack.

"What exactly are you doing here?" he asked finally. "What is it you want from us?"

Joshua hesitated as he pulled a wooden fife that had shiny metal tips at each end out of his hip pocket. "I want what you got. I want to go to school. Before, when this was a music-making room, I got my fife and joined right along with your band. 'Course, if someone played a note wrong, or one went sour, it liked to drive me crazy."

Danny couldn't help but smile, remembering Sophie's complaints when the toilet seat interrupted her trumpet solo.

"Even so," Joshua went on, "it sure was good listening to that music and learning them new songs. Now this here's a teaching room." He chuckled. "I figure now I can get me some knowledge."

Megan's mouth dropped in disbelief.

Danny could almost guess what Megan was thinking. Just as he did, she felt badly for Joshua and all the spirits forced from their special place when Crossfield's new wing was added. But a ghost in their band? A ghost in their bathroom? And now this ghost wanted to join them in the classroom? How would they manage that?

Megan glanced nervously at Danny while Joshua continued.

"Problem is, when you flesh-and-bloods raise your hands, your Ms. Hamilton calls on you. But if I raise my hand, no one sees. I have questions drumming inside my head. And it riles me to hear her sometimes give you wrong information about the war, even though it's not her fault. Some of those words in your learning book is not exactly as it was. It's missing certain important details—like how come this regiment or that stopped to mend a widow lady's root cellar with its trapdoor pried off, or to help a farmer birth his cow. But how would she know, not being there like I was?"

"Man." Danny pulled two chairs out of the classroom.

"Sounds like we need you," Megan said, sitting down on one chair while Joshua straddled the other and Danny sat cross-legged on the floor.

"Thanks." But Joshua wasn't finished. "And when your friend Biff raises two hands and jumps around like he has ants in his pants, you other flesh-and-bloods commence to laugh. Let *me* try to get attention, and your teacher slams the door in my face."

Danny grinned at Joshua's description of Biff and of Ms. Hamilton's reaction to an infuriatingly noisy toilet.

"Oh, so that's why you flush the toilet and make those loud noises!" Megan exclaimed. "Because you're stuck in this bathroom. Why on earth don't you come out?"

Joshua's eyes flashed. "Girl, this here is my special place. And don't you say I should find another. It's trickier than that. And I don't have time to explain. What I need is this here door open so I can hear the lesson and get my knowledge."

Whew! This ghost sure didn't ask for much.

"Honestly!" Megan pressed her fingers to her forehead. "This is all so strange. It's hard for me to imagine a war actually being fought here. I know there was one because of the Civil War markers and monuments around town. Even the names of our streets—"

"I think what she means is that it's hard to imagine this being anything other than a school," Danny said, jumping in. "You talk about a white house with green shutters, but all we know is Crossfield School and the playground and the brick houses in our neighborhood."

"You think Virginia is pretty now," Joshua said, as he put his fife safely away in his hip pocket. "You should have seen her then. There was a crick that meandered through woods back where the flagpole is."

"Is that where you got the water you gave me?" Danny asked.

"Yes. I was getting water for my friends when the shell exploded."

Suddenly, Joshua's face filled with the same look of horror Danny had seen through the videocamera.

"You don't have to go on," Danny said quickly. "I think I know. Or, at least, I know enough."

Joshua seemed relieved. "It's late. You should probably go on home."

Danny looked at his watch. "He's right. We've got to go, Megan. We've got school tomorrow."

"Not to mention the talent show," Megan added in case Danny had forgotten.

Danny turned to Joshua. "Are you going to be okay here?"

Joshua looked at his new friends and smiled. "Yes. I have been for a long time. But don't tell anyone you saw me. It would spoil everything."

"Are you sure?" Megan asked.

"What about Ms. Hamilton?" Danny asked.

Joshua held his hands up in front of his face. "No one. Not yet." His voice trailed like smoke in the air as he faded from view. "I beg you. Please."

Chapter 13

It was just his luck.

The next morning—the morning of the talent show—Danny had a goose egg the size of a grapefruit on his forehead from where he had banged his head on the toilet. It hurt like blazes. But the worst part was having to avoid Ms. Hamilton so she wouldn't see it.

Megan's note arrived on Danny's desk in the middle of math.

> Danny—
> I can't stop thinking about you know what
> and you know who. We promised we
> wouldn't tell, but it's so hard.
>
> Megan

Danny had just opened up Megan's note when Ms. Hamilton tapped him on the shoulder.

Uh-oh. It was too late to try covering it up with

his hand because she'd seen Danny open it.

"Is this something I should know about?" she asked.

"No, ma'am."

Danny gulped as their teacher bent closer and lifted his hair off his forehead with her pencil.

"That's quite a bump," she murmured. "Does this note have anything to do with it?"

He felt his eyes widen, as his face grew hot. "Oh, no, Ms. Hamilton. I fell off my bike. That's all."

"I don't know where you got that goose egg," Biff said to him in the cafeteria. "But you're not fooling me. In your entire life you have never fallen off your bike."

When Danny didn't respond, Biff winked at Sophie and Su Lin, who were in front of him in line. Then, casting a sidelong glance to make sure Danny was watching, he pretended to demolish a stack of trays with a chain saw.

"Rrrrrrreeeer."

He made a big show out of wiping the sweat off his forehead. "Wait till you and Megan see Su Lin and Sophie in my death-defying act this afternoon in the talent show. Don't tell the girls, but one of them might not make it out alive."

Danny gawked at Biff. Death defying? He shuddered. Wasn't one ghost enough?

Frantic, Danny tried to grab Biff, but Biff only shook him off as he cut ahead to join Tony and Matthew. Danny kept his eye on his friend as the three boys sat down.

Biff moved his arm back and forth over a table. Danny could almost hear the shrill whir of the blade. Then Biff grabbed his sides and cracked up. So did Tony and Matthew.

Feeling foolish, Danny stumbled toward the empty chair Megan had saved for him. For Sophie and Su Lin's sake, he could hope only one thing— that Biff wouldn't dare.

Unable to look at Biff, who was seated across from him, Danny was resting his head in his hands when Megan leaned closer to inspect his goose egg. Her hair brushed his cheek, and he blushed.

"Did you put ice on it like I told you?" she asked.

"Yeah. I went to sleep with a bag of frozen peas on my forehead." He leaned back in his chair and grinned sheepishly. "And then do you know what happened? I woke up with puddles in my eyeballs."

"You big goof." Megan crossed her green eye with her blue and sighed. "You're not supposed to go to sleep after you get hit in the head. I forgot to tell you that."

Unable to resist, Biff hooted, "Hey, you guys. Check out Danno's third eye. Cover up the other two and we can call him Cyclops. If that thing grows any bigger, he'll be a rhino-head."

The rest of the kids laughed—except for Megan, who stared Biff down with eyes narrowed into pinpricks until he all but cringed.

"Shut up!" Finished with Biff, Megan turned back to Danny. "What did your mother say?"

Danny shrugged. "I didn't let her see it."

Apparently, Biff wasn't in the mood to take orders from Megan. "Aw, poor baby. You didn't get your kissy-kissy this morning," he baited Danny in a loud singsongy voice. He waited until he had everyone's attention. "Danno's mommy kisses Danno smack on the forehead. Just like Snow White kissing the seven dwarfs. Hi-ho, hi-ho." Biff made a loud kissing noise on his arm.

Smack!

Danny blushed as Biff's voice rose even louder. "Maybe if Megan kissed it, it would make it better."

Megan was ignoring Biff. "So, who else's mom is coming to the talent show?" she asked everyone at the table. "My mom wouldn't miss it for the world."

Uh-oh, Danny thought to himself. Megan's tactic would never work. For Biff, being ignored was the ultimate insult. What would his friend do next? Danny wondered. He didn't have to wait long to find out.

Biff leaned across the table, coming closer and closer to Danny while making loud smooching noises in Danny's face. It was like Biff couldn't stop making a total fool out of himself.

Danny's temperature was rising fast. What was the matter with Biff? What about their secret pact?

Finally, Danny couldn't stand it any longer. "If you're not keeping your promise, I just might!" he yelled at Biff.

"Might what?" Biff shouted.

"Kiss Megan!" Danny hollered back without thinking.

He should have known better. What had happened was exactly what Biff wanted. Danny had never heard the cafeteria so quiet as he plopped back into his chair. Then everyone started to laugh, except for a few guys who whistled.

In his whole life, Danny had never felt like such a wreck. The bump on his head throbbed. His conscience prickled from keeping the secret about Joshua. His best friend was threatening to defy death with two of his classmates. And to top it off, he'd just announced to the whole world that he might kiss Megan McCarthy. What else could possibly go wrong?

The students, faculty, parents, and invited guests assembled outside the new wing at twelve-thirty. Mr. Barrie spoke for a few minutes, and then Dr. Pumphrey gave a long-winded speech before finally dedicating the new building.

At one-twenty, the children began filing into the auditorium.

"We're scheduled to perform last because our talent involves lowering the screen and using our projection video machine. It's a good thing our act is last," Megan whispered, as they took their places in the front section reserved for performers.

"I know what you mean," Danny mumbled.

Usually, he didn't get nervous when he gave a report. But standing on the stage in front of the entire student body—plus a reporter from the *Journal,* a bunch of parents, including his mom, and Dr.

Pumphrey—was different. By the time their turn rolled around, he'd probably feel as sick as Biff did on the Tower of Terror at Disney World.

Danny gritted his teeth as the first act took the stage—three tap dancers in red, white, and blue sequins, shuffling and tapping to "You're a Grand Old Flag." He couldn't blow it. Megan was depending on him.

A fourth grader who did bird calls came after the tap dancers. Later, four girls sang "Ding, Dong, the Wicked Witch Is Dead," followed by someone with a squeaky violin.

"I bet Joshua is crashing the toilet seat over this one," he murmured out of the side of his mouth.

"I meant to ask you," Megan whispered back. "Did you see him today?"

"No. Did you?"

Megan shook her head. "No. The bathroom was quiet, too. Do you think we scared him away?"

Danny mulled it over before answering. "I don't think so. Anyway, I hope not."

A few minutes later, a boy in a bright yellow jacket introduced his pet parrot to the audience. When the parrot refused to talk into the microphone, everyone applauded anyway—just as they applauded when a second grader played an unrecognizable "Row, Row, Row Your Boat" on the piano. They were getting near the end when Biff, Sophie, and Su Lin left their seats.

"Don't turn around now, but I just saw our mothers," Danny whispered to Megan. "And get this.

116

They're sitting next to each other! What do you want to bet that my mother finds out I wasn't at your house last night?"

"Right. And how much do you want to bet that we're both grounded for the rest of our lives? Let's try not to think about it."

Just at that moment The Great Bifferoni, the Magnificent Magician, swooped onto the stage with a flourish of his black-and-red satin cape, accompanied by two barefoot assistants dressed in flashy leotards and swirling pink-and-purple silk scarves.

"Wow!" Danny exclaimed. If he hadn't been expecting them, he never would have recognized Biff, Sophie, and Su Lin. They looked that professional.

While Su Lin swirled her scarves, Biff removed his white gloves, one finger at a time, and dropped them in his upturned top hat. Then, after tapping his hat twice with his magic wand, he handed it to Sophie, who spun around twice on her toes and tossed the hat upside down.

The gloves had disappeared!

Sophie handed the hat back to Biff. While everyone watched spellbound, Biff tapped the hat two more times. Then, after waving his hand over his hat and uttering a few magic words, he began pulling out scarves, eggs, a science book, and a stack of hall passes. When it seemed Biff could pull nothing else out of his hat, he reached inside and pulled out his white gloves.

Danny grinned with relief as he applauded. Since Biff was using harmless props, he wouldn't have to worry about Su Lin, Sophie, or chain saws. But just as Danny leaned back to relax and enjoy the rest of the show, Sophie shouted into the microphone.

"And now, ladies and gentlemen, boys and girls! The Great Bifferoni, the Magnificent Magician, will attempt a feat never before performed before a live audience."

Sophie's voice lowered. "Because of the death-defying nature of this act, The Great Bifferoni asks for complete silence."

Behind Sophie, two boys wheeled a large box to the middle of the stage while Biff shredded pieces of paper with a shiny silver sword. From where Danny was sitting, he couldn't tell—was Biff slicing paper or was it another trick? Was the sword fake, or was it real?

"One false slip of his razor-sharp sword," Sophie continued, "one small distraction, could mean certain death for Su Lin." She turned to Su Lin. "Are you ready?"

Together, Biff, Sophie, and Su Lin spun the box around so the audience could see all four of its elaborately decorated sides. Biff opened the box. Empty. Then he held his hand out to Su Lin, and as Danny watched, horrified, Su Lin stepped inside. Danny's heart skipped a tumultuous beat as Biff closed the box and locked it. Again, Biff and Sophie spun the box. Only this time, poor Su Lin was trapped inside!

Su Lin's coffin of death sat in the middle of the stage, while off to the side was a table with three bright, shiny swords. With a flourish of his cape, Biff strode toward the table. At the same time, Sophie turned to the audience and put a finger to her lips as a reminder.

Danny glanced from left to right. Was he the only one worried? Somebody ought to stop Biff before it was too late. Why didn't the teachers do something? What about Mr. Barrie or Dr. Pumphrey? They were smiling nervously in the first row.

Before Danny could move or even shout for help, Biff raised the first of his three swords and plunged it into the box.

"Owwww!" Su Lin's scream rang out through the auditorium.

Danny stiffened as Biff grabbed the second sword.

Thwump!

Every hair on Danny's neck stood straight up as another ear-piercing scream shot through the auditorium.

The Great Bifferoni appeared concerned. Danny glanced at Megan with alarm as the Magnificent Magician and his assistant approached the box.

"Whoops!" Biff exclaimed. "Ouch! That must have hurt."

Judging by the nervous way he was acting, it appeared Biff didn't know the microphone was picking up what he was saying. "Sorry, Su Lin. Did I miss again?"

"Eeewwww!" Kids in the front row squealed as red stuff oozed from the box.

Biff stared at the red puddle forming near his feet and grimaced. "Are you bleeding, Su Lin?" he asked.

"Not much," Su Lin responded weakly, although she continued to moan. "Are we almost finished?" she whimpered. Danny had to do something—fast. He was just about to race up the aisle when Biff paraded to the opposite side of the box, where he waved the third sword proudly in the air and jabbed it into Su Lin's coffin.

Suddenly, the moaning stopped.

But Biff wasn't finished. While Sophie danced around the stage with her scarves, he slowly and gruesomely removed the three swords one at a time. Then, after wiping the sweat off his forehead and pushing his cape back over his shoulder, he and Sophie unlocked the box.

He opened the door and stuck his hand in.

While the audience held its breath, Biff helped a smiling and uninjured Su Lin step out to take a bow. People were still clapping and stomping their feet in appreciation when Danny and Megan headed backstage. There was only one act between theirs and Biff's.

"Way to go, Biffer—" Danny stopped in mid-sentence. The crowd surrounding Biff was six deep. A photographer from the *Journal* was taking a picture of Biff, Sophie, and Su Lin, while a reporter wrote in a narrow spiral notebook. Danny gave Biff a thumbs up.

The Great Bifferoni, the Magnificent Magician, was a tough act to follow. A fourth-grade girl with butterfingers was playing the xylophone. The audience clapped politely at the end of her performance.

Danny nudged Megan. He motioned toward the audience with his head. "Don't worry. You'll win them back."

The expression on Megan's green-tinged face scared the living daylights out of him.

Meanwhile, behind them, Biff screamed. "Go out there and kill those guys! Go for it, M&M! You can do it, Danno."

If Megan heard, she didn't let on. She was standing in the middle of the stage staring straight ahead at nothing.

Danny had never seen Megan so scared. Not even when they'd confronted the haunted toilet in the dark.

"Ohmygosh, Danny!" she gasped hoarsely. "I don't think I can do this."

"Sure you can," Danny urged. "All you have to do is tell me when to dim the house lights. All eyes will focus directly on you."

It was the wrong thing to say.

Megan shook her head, struggling to get the words out, "You . . . don't understand . . . can't talk."

Danny stared at Megan, dumbstruck. So this was how it felt to pilot a wounded jetliner as it flew over the ocean at night.

"Hey, don't kid me about this!"

Megan's eyes filled. A tear rolled down her cheek.

Oh, no, a tiny voice screamed inside of him. *Don't do this to me.* He hated it when girls cried. What was he supposed to do?

Danny tried another track. "Shape up, Megan. Where's the big-deal actress? Think about it. We're Biff's only competition. The juggler dropped his dish, Myron's sideburns slipped, and the parrot pooped on his bicycle. Not only that, but I checked the tape last night. I checked it again this morning. Everything's perfect," he said, crossing his fingers behind him. "The tape is in the machine, ready to roll. All I need is your cue. You don't have a thing to worry about. Just read your poem."

Biting her lip, Megan nodded stiffly like a soldier going into a battle.

"Okay, kids. Curtain's going up," the stage manager called.

Danny stepped back into the shadows. Right before the curtains parted, Megan turned to him, smiled, and crossed her eyes—one blue, one green— for good luck. Danny's stomach churned. He had his finger ready at the switch as he whispered, "Hey, Meg. Break a leg."

Chapter 14

Danny pressed the button, and the auditorium was plunged into darkness. The audience gasped. There was no turning back now.

After a few awkward starts and skips, the spotlight finally found Megan. All the audience saw was the soft glow of her face, surrounded by inky blackness. You could have heard a pin drop, the audience was that quiet. Then she began.

"Bones," Megan recited in a loud, clear voice. "The title of my poem is 'Bones.'" She dragged the word out so it sounded like a gong. Danny had to hand it to Megan. She could be pretty dramatic.

Correction. Pretty *and* dramatic. He was so busy thinking about her, he almost missed his cue. He pressed another button on the wall, and the huge movie screen whirred downward, locking into position directly behind Megan. She took two steps stage left and nodded her chin. Immediately, Danny pressed the Play button on the VCR.

Megan couldn't help it. When a faint titter ran through the audience, she glanced nervously over her shoulder. They'd never counted on anyone thinking their phenomenally photogenic, perfectly choreographed background toilet might be funny. Then, with a haughty toss of her head, Megan resumed her reading.

It couldn't have been more perfect.

As Megan read the spooky poem, the toilet began to glow. In the front row, Mr. Barrie and Dr. Pumphrey leaned forward in their chairs.

Megan's voice rose. The toilet continued to glow brighter and brighter as Megan's poem reached its crescendo.

Finished, Megan stepped back into the shadows, as Danny began increasing the volume on the VCR. The only thing missing was popcorn. All eyes focused on the screen, where the mysterious toilet shone with a blinding, ghostly green light. Just then the urgent sounds of Danny protectively shoving Megan behind him blared through the speakers. A few seconds later, the camera began shaking. Now the mysterious toilet appeared more menacing than ever!

Suddenly, the camera jerked abruptly to a shot of the bathroom wall. Finally, Danny's crumpled body lying on the floor in front of the toilet flashed on the screen while Megan screamed, "Oh, no! Somebody, help. Please! Heeelp!" Actresses got awards for performances like that!

When the tape cut off and the house lights came up, the audience went wild.

Backstage, Megan's eyes were the shiniest blue and green Danny had ever seen. At that very second, he almost broke the pact he'd made with Biff and kissed her. But Megan had started dancing a silly jig, and, as everybody knows, a moving target is almost impossible to kiss.

"Yes!" Danny whooped. Instead of a kiss, he gave Megan two thumbs up.

"We did it! They really liked us. We're the last act. I bet all the judges vote for us!" Megan was so excited, her words tumbled over each other as she tried to shout above the thunderous applause. Then she threw her poem up in the air. When the paper fluttered to the floor, she and Danny were practically nose to nose.

Danny stared into those shiny pools of blue and green for the second time in less than a minute and gulped. Flustered, he grabbed the curtains and stuck his head through the opening.

"Hey!" he yelled. "Where are Mr. Barrie and Dr. Pumphrey?!"

Their seats were empty!

"Ohmygosh! The toilet!" Megan whispered hoarsely.

"Joshua! We've got to warn him! Quick, the back door's faster!" Danny pushed tables and props aside. "We have to get to the bathroom before they do!"

Danny and Megan raced down the hallway to Room Fifteen. They thundered through the classroom door, and—

Too late!

Completely helpless, Danny and Megan watched silently as Dr. Pumphrey scratched the toilet bowl with a key. Afterward, he rubbed the key between his fingers and frowned. "That's funny. I could have sworn those kids used phosphorescent paint," he told Mr. Barrie.

"Obviously they did something," Mr. Barrie mused out loud.

"Excuse me," Ms. Hamilton interrupted. "But these are good kids. They're both in my class and are excellent students. I don't believe either of them would deface school property."

Busy ogling the toilet, none of the grown-ups noticed the slim wooden object lying in the far corner.

Danny jabbed Megan with his elbow. Joshua's fife!

Instinctively, Danny knew. Joshua had left his flesh-and-blood friends the ammunition they needed to get themselves out of trouble. Loyal to the end, even if it meant he would lose his special place, Joshua was trying to save his friends.

Danny couldn't let it happen. He'd say it was an emergency, that he had to throw up and needed to use the toilet. He'd shut the door, grab the fife, and stuff it under his shirt.

But he never had a chance.

"Danny Adams and Megan McCarthy, I believe." Mr. Barrie cocked his head and raised his left eyebrow. "We'll discuss this situation in my office after today's classes are dismissed. You might be wise to ask your mothers to stay."

With that statement, the two men were gone. In the same instant, Ms. Hamilton glided into the bathroom and scooped up the fife. With a sidelong, questioning glance in Danny and Megan's direction, she carefully placed it in her desk drawer.

"Well!" Ms. Hamilton exclaimed. "That spectacle of yours certainly blew absolutely everyone out of their seats. When exactly did you make that video, Danny?"

"Last night," Danny mumbled.

"But it was the only time we could do it. And the school was open," Megan added. "It wasn't breaking and entering. We didn't even have to crawl through a window or do anything illegal."

Ms. Hamilton shook her finger and pointed at each of them. "But you were still in the building without permission. That's a security violation."

"We didn't do anything to the toilet," Megan and Danny wailed with one voice.

"Hold it right there!" Ms. Hamilton said, looking around. "In all the excitement, I left my purse on my chair in the auditorium. Don't move. I'll be right back," she said, running out of the room.

An inexplicable feeling made Danny suddenly turn. Joshua was casually leaning against the bathroom door.

"Oh, you're here," Megan whispered.

Joshua nodded. "I've been here all along. I decided you can tell your teacher. That's why I left my fife."

"Smart thinking," Danny agreed. "She's a good

person to have on your side. She already knows an awful lot about the Civil War. Maybe not as much as you do, but she still knows a lot."

"I even think she'll keep your secret," Megan said.

"Let's hope so," Joshua whispered, as he began fading from sight. "Because I still do want some education."

"Well," Ms. Hamilton said when she returned, as she set her purse down on the desk. "The judges are still deliberating and our student orchestra, mercy me, is about to repeat their program. I'll leave this hall door open, and when the band stops, we'll know to go back for the results."

Megan cleared her throat. "Ms. Hamilton, Danny and I have something incredible to tell you."

"Yes, but first you'd better sit down," Danny added.

Ms. Hamilton pulled out her chair. "I'll bet it has something to do with my Civil War shawl that I found early this morning in the bathroom. Hmm, Megan? And the fife I discovered a few minutes ago, Danny?" Her forehead wrinkling, she examined both of them with her eyes.

"Perhaps you should tell me. Who exactly is Joshua?"

Chapter 15

Not even stopping to wonder how his teacher knew Joshua's name, Danny spoke rapidly: "Joshua's a ghost. He's our age, he lives in the bathroom, and he wants to be in our class."

"He's from the Civil War. We both saw him," Megan proclaimed, as she moved closer to the teacher.

Ms. Hamilton looked at Danny and Megan for a moment. She opened her desk drawer and reached inside. "This fife has the name *Joshua* carved into it. Does it belong to him?"

"Yes," Danny said excitedly. "Joshua told us what happened here during the war. Of course, we already knew about the battles. But we didn't know about the big white house with a wide porch. And there was a creek running near the flagpole that was cool and shady and pretty. And that's not all, Ms. Hamilton!" Danny exclaimed. "There wasn't any hospital near here, so when a bunch of soldiers got hurt in a skirmish, the others carried them to the house with the porch. It was right where the new wing is now!"

Megan poked him on the shoulder. "Danny, she wants to know about Joshua!"

Danny didn't need to be urged. It was just that there was so much to tell. How do you decide what to say first? He took a deep breath. "Joshua had filled his canteen with water and was on his way back to his wounded friends when he got killed. He and his spirit friends have been hanging around here ever since. Do you believe us, Ms. Hamilton?"

Ms. Hamilton laughed nervously. "You know, actually, I think I do. There were ghosts in my sorority house at college. In fact, some people believe that many of the older homes in Charlottesville have ghosts." Ms. Hamilton turned the fife over in her hand, examining it thoughtfully. "We can check Joshua's facts about the battle easily enough in our county records. It'll be a good research project."

"So," Megan said. "You'll leave the bathroom door open?"

"I don't see why not. In my twelve years of teaching, I've encountered many things, but never a ghost. This will certainly be a challenge."

"You can't tell anyone, though," Danny reminded her. "Joshua doesn't want any other flesh-and-bloods to know except the three of us."

Ms. Hamilton smiled. "Joshua doesn't have to worry about that. Having a ghost in our school would spook Mr. Barrie for sure, and I'd hate to think what it might do to Superintendent Pumphrey." Ms. Hamilton stood up and began to pace across the front of the room. "You two still have to face them after school. I'll do whatever I can, but be prepared for some severe consequences." She paused and looked directly at them. "It's very possible that Mr. Barrie will ask you to turn in your patrol belts."

Danny grimaced and muttered to himself.

"Maybe it won't be forever," Megan consoled, patting him on the arm. "We didn't hurt anything."

Just then the music stopped. Megan looked at Danny, and they both looked at Ms. Hamilton. The judges had decided. The award ceremony would start in a few minutes.

"Hurry," Ms. Hamilton urged. "You should be on stage with the rest of the performers. Regardless of who wins, the two of you deserve recognition for your outstanding production."

If anyone had asked Danny, he would have said that having all of the kids on stage at the same time was definitely not a good idea. There simply wasn't enough room. Besides that, there were too many animals. Even as the stage manager herded everyone into place, a black-and-white dog in a clown hat growled at a hyperactive gerbil.

"Hey, move, would you," a girl snarled. "You're stepping on my cat's leash."

Meanwhile, clustered near Megan's elbow, four

girls in pigtails began singing in high-pitched squeaky voices.

"Cut it out," the boy beside Danny growled. "If I hear 'Ding, Dong, the Wicked Witch Is Dead' one more time, I'm going to puke."

"You will not!"

"Will too."

"Has anyone seen my boa constrictor?"

"You lost your boa constrictor?" the boy with the gerbil shrieked.

"I dare ya to sing it again," taunted one of the pigtailed girls.

"I double dare ya," said another.

"Ding, dong, the wicked witch is dead," all four sang in full chorus.

Prepared for the worst, Danny tried to step back, but they were jammed too close together. Nobody was going anywhere.

Myron, in his silver jumpsuit, dark glasses, and black caterpillar sideburns, snapped his fingers and plunked a string on his guitar. "The boa constrictor was a fake. Let it go, brother," he twanged, in his best Elvis imitation. It was all the parrot needed.

"Brother! Brother! Let it go!" the parrot squawked.

"See! I told you Pauli could talk," the little boy in the yellow jacket screamed. He turned to his parrot. "Pauli! Why didn't you do that before?"

But Pauli wasn't paying attention. He was too busy zeroing in on the fuzzy black sideburns. Suddenly, a pair of green wings spread monstrously wide. With a gigantic flap, the bird lunged at Myron's left cheek.

Myron threw his arms protectively to his face, as he and a bunch of other kids fell flailing to the floor.

"Help! Attack parrot!" someone screamed, obviously referring to Pauli, who only wanted a taste of caterpillar sideburns.

But the damage was done.

Panic-stricken, a first grader started crying for his mommy, while the rest of the kids started shoving, trying to get away. Who could possibly know what the parrot might attack next?

Then, just when Danny thought it couldn't possibly get worse, it did—the heavy velvet curtains sliding noisily on the tracks overhead startled poor Pauli, who swooped and pooped into the audience. While the kids pointed and yelled, the parrot circled the entire auditorium, squawking and flapping and sending tiny green feathers and a few other gifts drifting into the crowd below. Finally the petrified parrot landed on a loud speaker box.

What a disaster! It took forever for Mr. Barrie and the teachers to get everyone and everything back under control. It was only then that Mr. Barrie waved his arms and made the long-awaited announcement.

"The winning act is . . . The Great Bifferoni, the Magnificent Magician!"

If Danny had not seen it for himself, he wouldn't

have believed it. For all of Biff's big talk about being the best, he actually appeared surprised to have won first prize.

"Biff. Biff?" Mr. Barrie summoned Biff forward. "Come and get your trophy."

Then, wonder of wonders, instead of running across the stage and approaching the microphone alone, Biff graciously turned and gestured to Sophie and Su Lin to go first.

The audience was applauding loudly, with Danny and Megan clapping loudest of all.

As the audience started to calm down, Mr. Barrie tapped the microphone with his finger and cleared his throat. "The second-place trophy goes to Danny Adams, Megan McCarthy, and the Mysterious Haunted Toilet."

The kids went wild as Danny, Biff, Megan, Su Lin, and Sophie all slapped hands in a series of high fives.

Later that afternoon, shoulders slumped and heels dragging, Danny entered the principal's office along with Megan. Their mothers were already there, seated on the bench near the window.

Only a few short minutes before, Danny and Megan had been celebrating their victory. Now Danny felt like the weight of the world had been dropped on his shoulders. His father wasn't going to be happy if his son got suspended from school.

Mr. Barrie was drumming his fingers on his desk,

as Danny and Megan sat down to face him. A firing squad would have been more pleasant.

Swallowing was impossible. Danny stared at his hands, clasped in his lap. He and Megan were going to get kicked out of school for sure.

But then Mr. Barrie surprised them.

"I realize that you're wearing your patrol belts, but that won't be necessary anymore," Mr. Barrie said, as he reached his open hand across the desk. "Would the two of you please remove your patrol belts and give them to me."

The way Mr. Barrie said it, it wasn't a question.

Danny fumbled nervously with the buckle. Out of the corner of his eye, he could see Megan was having trouble, too.

"I hope you both know that what you did is extremely serious," Mr. Barrie continued, looking sterner than ever. He took the belts and set them aside. "You are not to be on school property after hours without permission. Is that clear?"

"Yes, sir," Danny and Megan said together.

"We're sorry," Megan said meekly.

"We won't ever do it again," Danny added, just in case his mother or Mr. Barrie had any doubts.

Mr. Barrie nodded at their moms before returning his gaze to Danny and Megan. "I'm putting the two of you on probation. If you can show your usual good and responsible behavior for the next four weeks, I'll see about having you reinstated as patrols. But your behavior must be exemplary."

"Yes, sir!" Megan almost bolted from her chair.

At the same time, Danny couldn't help but smile to himself. Maybe getting into trouble wasn't such a bad thing. With any luck, he and Megan might even share the same intersection when they got their new patrol assignments.

Chapter 16

No longer an active patrol, Danny arrived at school earlier than usual the following Monday, to discover a small basket of books in the bathroom. Some were the kind with big print and short sentences. Others had lots of pictures.

"Are the books for Joshua?" he whispered to Megan in between classes.

"Probably. Did you see how Ms. Hamilton left the bathroom door open? Whatever we discuss in class, Joshua is sure to hear."

That day the class noticed fewer eruptions, much quieter splutterings, and only an occasional dropped seat from the bathroom.

"Now that the remodeling is finished, I guess the toilet won't act up anymore," Sophie said at lunch.

Megan raised her eyebrows at Danny, and he smiled back at her secretively.

On Tuesday, after morning announcements, Ms. Hamilton stood in front of the class, her face glowing with pleasure. "Now that the excitement of the talent show has passed, we can begin devoting our energies to our Civil War unit, culminating in our play. And just to get everyone in the mood," she said, as she began walking slowly toward the back of the room, "I'll begin setting my Civil War collectibles and other important items out where you can all study and appreciate them."

When she said the word "all," Ms. Hamilton turned slightly toward the bathroom. Danny covered his grin with his hand.

Later that afternoon, while the other kids were busy writing in their science journals, Danny noticed Ms. Hamilton creating a display on the empty table at the back of the room. He cleared his throat to signal Megan, who cocked her eyebrow quizzically as their teacher draped her shawl over a nearby chair.

No one else seemed very interested in the display, but Danny was excited. Right before dismissal, he checked one of the items Ms. Hamilton had left on the table. It was the Civil War book with the blue-and-gray cover with faded red stars. Danny made sure to note what page it was opened to: page twenty-two.

The next morning, he headed straight for the book. It had been turned to page twenty-five. When he looked up, Ms. Hamilton only nodded and smiled. Then she moved some of her Civil War items to different locations in the classroom.

"It's like she's luring a kitten out from under a

bed," Megan told Danny that evening on the phone.

"I don't think she likes the idea of Joshua feeling trapped in the bathroom all the time," Danny commented. "She wants him to join us in the classroom."

"And after she gets him into our classroom, then what will she do?"

"Beats me," Danny answered.

On Thursday, right before lunch, Ms. Hamilton added the final touch. She opened her drawer and placed Joshua's fife on her desk. Seeing it, Danny caught his breath. What would Joshua's reaction be now? Danny didn't have to wait long to find out. When they returned after lunch, the fife was still on the teacher's desk—but it had been turned around. No one had been in the classroom—except Joshua!

It was the perfect moment for Ms. Hamilton to make another announcement about their Civil War play.

"This year's play will be completely different from previous performances," Ms. Hamilton told the class. "Part of education, part of being a reader and a writer, is learning new things and opening the doors to new adventures."

She nodded toward the bathroom door and winked first at Danny and then at Megan before continuing to address the rest of the class.

"Recently, two of your classmates, Danny Adams and Megan McCarthy, discovered that a real Civil War skirmish took place right here where Crossfield School is." Ms. Hamilton paused, allowing a buzz of excitement to travel through the room. "I'd like our play to be about that event."

Biff raised his hand. "How? We don't know anything about that."

"Yeah. What's a skirmish anyway?" someone asked.

"A skirmish is a minor battle," Ms. Hamilton explained, as she wrote "The Skirmish of Crossfield Creek" on the chalkboard. "By the time we're finished, we'll know what happened here on this very site. Megan and Danny volunteered to research the battle and help write the play."

Danny smiled to himself. Obviously as part of their research, Ms. Hamilton meant for them to interview Joshua. Cool. He, Megan, and Joshua would have a great time. Two flesh-and-bloods and one ghostwriter!

As if to agree, a satisfied-sounding gurgle came from the toilet.

"It's okay, Dad. Really," Danny said into the phone on Sunday.

His Dad was asking about the talent show, which by then was old news—not nearly as exciting as what Danny wanted to talk about.

"First place is nice, but second was good, too," Danny said. "Besides, Biff's been perfecting his magic act for years. He deserved to win. You know how he used to make those gross noises? He's not doing it anymore. Now he's concentrating all of his energy on real magic and being a good patrol captain."

"Well, that's excellent, Danny," his dad said.

"Next month, Biff wants me to tape a video of him levitating his new baby brother—or sister," Danny went on. "He's going to try it in the hospital as soon as the baby's born. Right through the hospital glass." Danny balanced the phone between his ear and his shoulder while unscrewing the cap on a peanut butter jar. "Cool, huh, Dad?"

Mr. Adams laughed. "That should make Biff good and famous."

Danny laughed, too. "I don't mind. Besides, Mom says what I'm doing is more important. Did she tell you? I'm the new official photographer for our Civil War play, which, by the way, Megan and I are writing at Ms. Hamilton's request."

"Congratulations! Now, that's really impressive." Danny could almost see his dad beam.

"Yeah, Megan and I discovered that there was a Civil War skirmish right where the new wing of Crossfield School was built. The Skirmish of Crossfield Creek. That's what the play and film are going to be about. And that's not all."

"There's more?" His dad sounded surprised and pleased.

"Yeah, Dad. Afterward, the film is going to be put in the county library. People will be able to check it out, same as a book. Cool, huh?"

"Very. I'm proud of you, son."

Even as Danny basked in his father's praise, he eyed the wooden fife Joshua had allowed him to bring home. When he and Megan were finished,

Joshua would be able to rest easy, knowing that the people in their community would appreciate all that Joshua and his friends had endured that hot day in August, the third summer of the Civil War.